ANGEL

DADDIES OF THE SHADOWS
BOOK 9

KATE OLIVER

ACKNOWLEDGMENTS

To my amazing readers,

I just want to take a moment to say thank you. When I started this series, I had no idea how much you all would love this family and it has been such a pleasure bringing each character to life for you. Even though we still have Tate coming, with this being the last brother in the series, I'm feeling overwhelmed with emotions. I've fallen in love with these Daddies and Littles as much as you have. I hope you'll love my Mafia Daddies (Syndicate Kings) and Small Town Daddies (Daddies of Pine Hollow) just as much as you've loved these guys.

I'm grateful to each and every one of you. The reviews, comments, emails, messages, posts, shares, and everything else you all do. It never goes unnoticed, and I hope you all can feel just how much I love you because I truly do.

I want to also take a moment to thank the people who have helped me throughout this series. Rose Chaplan, Rhonda Butterbaugh, Pat Bernal Johnston, Becca Jameson, Cheryl Maddox, Sara Dreps Titus, my entire amazing ARC team, and my wonderfully patient husband who has to listen to me talking about my characters like they are my family. Thank you so much. I love you guys and I couldn't do it without you!

This isn't goodbye to the Daddies of the Shadows. It's see ya later, alligator.

Love, Kate

TRIGGER WARNINGS

This book is a Daddy Dom, little girl, age play romance. Age play falls under the BDSM umbrella. The MMC in this book is a Daddy Dom and the MFC identifies as a Little. This is an act of role-playing between the characters. This is a consensual power exchange relationship between adults. In this story there are spankings and discussions of other forms of discipline. The MFC also wears adult diapers and uses a pacifier, and sippy cup in this story.

In Angel's story, there is discussion of past abuse to a minor, both sexual and physical.

Please do not read this story if you find any of this to be disturbing or a trigger for you.

PROLOGUE
ANGEL

"Hello?"

Angel watched the face of his brother's fiancée turn from happy to horrified as she listened to whoever was on the other end of the phone. Hawk was hovering close to Ellie and when she turned to look up at him, he nodded.

"Yes, of course. How far away are you? Are you okay?"

Ellie's eyes widened and then filled with tears. "He hit you? Oh my god! What? Oh, Nora. Where are you? Do we need to come get you?"

The rest of what Ellie said to her friend was lost on him. He was too busy fighting the rage inside. He didn't even know her best friend, Nora, and he wanted to hunt down the motherfucker who'd hurt her and kill him. Angel could tolerate a lot of things, but he never tolerated abuse.

He felt a set of eyes on him, and looked down to find Ellie staring up at him with tears running down her cheeks. That's when he made her a promise he had every intention of keeping.

"We'll take care of her, Little girl. She's one of us now. Whoever hurt her is dead."

1

NORA

W hy was she so stupid? What had she even been thinking? She couldn't help but silently berate herself for her naïveté, for being so desperate to find a Daddy to belong to that she had let herself believe he loved her. She'd thought he actually wanted her and that he would be the perfect Daddy she'd always dreamed about. Not only had she been wrong, she'd been horribly wrong. The realization was like a knife in her gut. Tears welled up in her eyes as she struggled to come to terms with the painful truth.

Lifting her hand to the bruise on her cheek, she winced. Her relationship with Trevor had been over for months, but she'd been trying to make it work, trying to be better so he would want her again, but really, she didn't even know why she'd tried. She hadn't been in love with him for months. She'd quickly fallen out of love with him when she'd found out he'd been cheating on her. She was just so pathetic and needy that she'd put up with it all and tried to make it work.

After their most recent fight, where he'd hit her with his

closed fist and given her a swollen and bruised cheek, she'd finally decided it was time to get out. She just hated that the only place she had to go was her best friend's house. Not that she didn't want to see Ellie, because she did. She could hardly wait to see her. Since Nora had moved away from Seattle, they hadn't been able to talk as much as they typically did. Her bestie was in a new relationship with a Daddy of her own, and she didn't want to interfere with the new life she had. And the idea of being around Ellie's new Daddy, or any man, for that matter, was absolutely terrifying.

Strangers of any kind terrified her. Heck, even people she knew scared her. Just because you know somebody doesn't mean they are trustworthy or safe. She'd learned that lesson way too many times throughout her life.

At her age, she thought she would have grown out of her fears and shyness, but it almost seemed to get worse the older she got. Ellie said he would understand but she was sure he would think she was a freak. Just like Trevor said she was.

The automated voice on her GPS told her to turn and when she did, she nearly choked. The row of houses on each side of the street were gorgeous. Huge, custom houses with pristine yards lined with trimmed bushes and flowerbeds. This couldn't be right. Could it?

Bringing her car to a stop, she looked down at her phone to double-check the address Ellie had sent her. According to that, she was in the right place. She pulled over to the side of the road, put her car in park, and stared up at the massive house.

Before she could even gather her bearings, Ellie emerged from the front door with a very large, bald man right behind her. He stayed on the porch as she bounded down the driveway toward the car. Opening her door, Nora hesitantly got out and was instantly wrapped up in a hug by her best friend in the whole world.

"I missed you so much. I'm so glad you're here," Ellie whispered.

Letting out a deep breath, Nora hugged her back. "I missed you, too."

When they released each other and Ellie caught a glimpse of her face, she gasped. "Oh, my God! Nora, oh, shit. We need to get ice on your cheek. It's swollen and red. What did he do to you? Come inside and le—"

Shaking her head, she looked up at the looming man on the porch and shuddered. "I'm okay. I promise. I should get a hotel."

Ellie knew her better than anyone. "I promise you're safe here. He knows you're shy and it's okay if you don't talk to him. Hawk is... intimidating, but he will protect you with his life or die trying if it comes to that. We want you here where you're safe."

Nora trusted her best friend more than anyone. After all, Ellie had been there for her when she'd gone through some of the darkest days of her life. They were closer than friends. They were family. Even if they weren't actually related.

Taking a deep breath, Nora nodded and took the hand that Ellie was offering, following her toward the porch. Ellie stopped in front of the massive man and smiled. "This is Nora. Nora, this is Hawk."

She froze, unable to smile or wave or speak. This always happened. Anytime she met someone new, she froze. And it was no different with this beast of a man, though Ellie didn't seem the least bit fazed by his intimidating presence. His dark eyes burned into hers, but she couldn't look away from them. She also couldn't speak so she just stood there looking like an idiot like she always did. Thankfully, Hawk just smiled at her and motioned for the women to go inside.

As soon as Nora walked into the house, she felt a wave of relief wash over her. She was safe here. It was an inexplicable feeling but one she couldn't deny. Ellie led her down a hall that opened up into a large living room, complete with plush seating and tasteful décor on the walls. The living room transitioned into a beautiful kitchen. As soon as they walked in, a cute little dog came bounding up to Nora, her tail wagging furiously. Smiling, she reached down to stroke the dog's fur, which was silky beneath her fingertips. It reminded her of some of her beloved stuffies she'd left behind, but the warmth and wiggly energy of the dog, coupled with its expressive eyes, soothed her on the inside.

Ellie went into the kitchen and opened the fridge, then brought her an ice pack. "Put this on your cheek."

Hawk followed them inside and stood awkwardly off to the side. Nora sensed he wanted to say something, but he stayed quiet. The only noise she heard from him was a low growl when she brought the ice pack to her cheek and winced.

"Sit down. Do you want something to drink? Maybe we should call the doctor. Daddy, should we call the doctor?" Ellie asked.

"Yeah, I think I'll send him a message. If anything, he can recommend something to help with the bruising and swelling," Hawk answered, his voice deep and stern.

Shaking her head at Ellie, she could feel her eyes widen. "No. I'm okay," she whispered.

"I'm calling the doctor and that's final," Hawk replied before he disappeared from the room.

Ellie rolled her eyes and shook her head. "I know he

seems really scary, but he means well and his heart is pure gold."

Nora wasn't so sure about that. She'd thought Trevor was sweet and had a good heart, but she'd learned that terrible lesson. She should have known better. There was a reason she always kept to herself. It was the only way not to get hurt.

"How long has this been going on, Nora? Has he hit you before? Hawk and his brothers are going apeshit trying to get information from me about him so they can find him and teach him a lesson."

Her eyes widened even farther. "No. They can't. He's dangerous, Ellie. Just leave it alone. I'm here now."

Hawk's deep voice startled her. "We're not leaving anything alone. We don't tolerate abusers. We take care of our own, and you are now one of us, Little one."

Chewing on her bottom lip, she shot Ellie a pleading look. God, Hawk probably already thought she was insane. Why couldn't she just talk to people like a normal person? Why did she have to be so strange?

Because that's how you survived this long in the world.

The sound of the front door opening and closing made her freeze and tense up. Within seconds, a tall, tanned, tattooed, and ridiculously muscular man walked into the living room. His almost black eyes looked at Hawk before they landed on her, and she could swear she stopped breathing completely as he stared at her.

"You must be Nora," he growled in a low voice.

Goosebumps rose over her flesh and she couldn't do anything but stare back at him as he studied her face, his eyes darkening even more as he looked at the ice pack she held up to her cheek.

"This is Angel. He's Hawk's brother. Angel, this is my bestie, Nora," Ellie introduced.

Angel nodded and offered her a soft, reassuring smile that warmed her from the inside out. Why was she having such a reaction to this man? He looked terrifying but for whatever reason, she took comfort in that.

The sound of the door opening again made her tense all over again. How many people were going to come in? Her breathing turned shallow at the thought of a bunch of strangers around her. Without saying anything, Angel moved closer to her. Had he noticed her reaction? He probably thought she was weird.

Lowering the ice pack from her face, she brought it down to her lap and stared at her hands nervously.

"Put that back on your cheek, Little one," Angel told her softly.

Without thinking, she immediately obeyed his command just as another even larger man with a full beard and dark hair walked into the room with a tiny woman next to him. The woman was dressed all in pink with a big bow at the base of her high ponytail.

"Is she here? Has she told us where this motherfucker lives?" the large, hairy man asked.

Angel shook his head. "She's right fucking here, you dipshit. Fuck, look around the room before you start asking questions."

Nora shrank back onto the couch as the hairy man's gaze zeroed in on her.

Angel turned to her and raised his eyebrows. "Ice pack back on your face, Nora. Do you need me to hold it there?"

Letting out a gasp, she raised the cold pack again and shook her head. Thankfully, Ellie spoke up for her.

"Guys, everyone needs to calm down. Nora is really shy and she just got here."

Hawk nodded. "Tate is on his way to take a look at her

cheek and any other injuries she might have. After we get her taken care of, we will go from there."

Huh, maybe the beast of a man wasn't so bad after all. Except, had he just said someone was coming to check her out? A doctor? There was no way in hell she was going to see a doctor. No. Nope. Not happening. No way in hell.

Tugging on Ellie's hand, Nora leaned over and whispered in her ear. "I'm not seeing a doctor. You know I can't. I'll freak out."

Ellie nibbled on her bottom lip as she looked up at Hawk. "Daddy, she doesn't want to see a doctor. She's...uh, she doesn't like doctors."

2

ANGEL

Like hell she wasn't seeing a goddamn doctor. Her cheek was multiple shades of purple and swollen. Who knew what other injuries she had. Jesus fuck, the guy who hurt her was going to die a very painful and drawn out death.

The second he'd walked into Hawk's house and laid eyes on Nora, he knew she was his. Fuck, he'd pretty much known it from the first time he'd heard her voice over the phone when she'd called Ellie one time.

Now, seeing her in person, seeing the fear in her eyes, made the rage inside him burn like a wildfire. He wanted to go hunting for blood. He would find his prey and that prey would meet the savage that Angel kept pushed down deep inside himself.

"She's seeing the doctor," Angel said firmly.

Nora looked up at him with a pleading look, slowly shaking her head. Her hand crept up to her mouth and he wondered if she wanted to suck her thumb.

Kneeling in front of her so he was more at her level, he stared into her deep green eyes. "I know it's scary seeing

12

doctors, but we just want to make sure you're okay. The doctor that's coming is a close friend who we trust completely, and I'll make sure he doesn't do anything to scare you. Can you be brave for us, please?"

Even though he was asking, it wasn't something he'd allow her to say no to. She didn't know him and he didn't know her, but the health and safety of women were the most important things to him. Making sure she didn't need to go to the hospital was something he wouldn't budge on. His brothers wouldn't, either. But she was terrified and he needed to make it seem like it was her choice to see the doctor.

She nibbled on her lip and sighed softly. The poor sweet thing was exhausted. He could see it in her eyes. Exhausted and scared. Who knew how long she'd been putting up with the abuse she'd endured before she finally got away. One thing he knew without a doubt was that she would never go through that kind of pain again. Whether she liked it or not, she was under his family's protection now.

"'Kay," she whispered so quietly he barely heard her.

Smiling at her, he nodded. "Good girl."

Lucy walked over to the couch and plopped down next to Ellie, smiling widely at Nora. "Hi. I'm Lucy. My Daddy is Hawk's brother."

Nora nodded at Lucy. Ellie had warned them all before Nora had arrived that she was shy, but he hadn't expected her to be quite as shy as she was. It was hard because he wanted to drill her with questions, declare that she was his, and move her into his house right this fucking second. He could tell none of those things would be happening that quickly.

It was probably crazy of him to know that she was his, but he did, and he didn't give a fuck about crazy. Therapists had told him for years that he was crazy— they didn't use that term exactly, but he knew that was the translation— and finally, he stopped trying to get help and embraced his crazy side because, fuck it. His family loved him for who he was and that was the only thing in the world that mattered to him. He just hoped Nora would learn to love that side of him. He'd done a good job of pushing his rage and crazy deep down inside for the past twenty years or so, but it was still there, and very rarely did he let it come out to play.

Someone rang the doorbell and he watched as she visibly tensed just as she had when Wolf and Lucy had walked in the house. No woman or person, for that matter, should ever be that afraid. It made him want to pick her up from the couch and rock her in his arms to soothe her, but he was pretty sure at this point, it would freak her out even more, so he stayed where he was, kneeling right in front of her, a safe distance away so she didn't feel too crowded.

Hawk left the room to answer the door and appeared a moment later with Tate following behind with his doctor's bag in hand. Nora immediately started trembling, causing Angel to rise up and turn to Tate, stopping the older man in his tracks with just his expression. When he realized how rapidly she was breathing, he turned back to everyone in the room. "Maybe we need to clear out the room and give Nora some space."

Wolf nodded. "Sure. Come on, Lucy. Let's go get groceries and maybe we can stop by later once Nora is settled."

Lucy stood from the couch and smiled softly at Nora. "It was so nice to finally meet you. I can't wait to hang out more. We'll be besties in no time."

Bless Lucy and her optimism. She could be such a sweetheart when she wanted to be.

Tate stood off to the side while Wolf and Lucy left.

When they were gone, Angel pointed toward the doctor. "This is Tate. He's a doctor and he's our friend. He's very kind and gentle, but if he were to ever do anything to hurt you, I'd kill him with my bare hands."

Okay, maybe he shouldn't have said that. Her eyes widened as she glanced at Tate, who was smiling and shaking his head.

"Don't worry, Nora. I'm pretty sure each of these guys has threatened to kill me at one time or another if I ever hurt their Little girl," Tate told her. "I see you have an owwie there on your cheek. Would it be okay if I came near you to take a look at it? I promise not to touch."

Angel kept his gaze on her as Tate talked and when he finished, she glanced at Angel who nodded and smiled as reassuringly as he could. He didn't know why but even though she'd only said one word to him since he'd been there, she seemed to search him out in the room more than anyone else.

She looked back at Tate and nodded. Tate smiled and walked over to where Angel had sat down. "Move."

Rolling his eyes at the Doc, Angel got up and moved away from them, but only a few feet. He wanted to stay as close as he could to Nora without scaring her. She was like a magnet to him.

Tate sat down on the coffee table across from her, opened his bag, and dug around in it for a minute before he pulled out a tiny stuffed bear wearing doctor's scrubs and a stethoscope around its neck. He held it up for Nora. "I've had this little guy in my bag for a while now. Would you like to hold him while I look at your cheek?"

Nora eyed the small bear and then nodded, taking it delicately from Tate's hands.

"Thank you. Now, can you remove the ice pack so I can see your cheek?"

Angel stood silently as she lowered the pack from her face and when he saw the bruise again, he let out a low growl that had her looking over at him in alarm.

"Sorry, Little one. I didn't mean to frighten you. I just hate seeing you hurt," Angel reassured her.

Shaking his head, Tate grimaced. "I swear this family is secretly a bunch of wolf shifters that can't stop growling all the time."

To Angel's surprise, Nora giggled, and it was the sweetest fucking sound he'd ever heard in his life. Damn, he really wanted to kill Tate for being the one to make her laugh.

"Nora, can you open your mouth and stick your tongue out for me?" Tate asked.

She hesitated briefly but complied with his request. Tate did as he promised and kept his distance as he shone a tiny light into her mouth. When he was done, he nodded. "Thank you. I'd like to look inside your ears to make sure you don't have any tissue or ear drum damage. I'll need to get a little closer with my tool to be able to do that. Would that be okay with you?"

When she glanced up at Angel again, he smiled softly and nodded. Fuck, he felt like he was on top of the world every time she looked to him for approval. Even though Ellie was still sitting on the couch right next to Nora, she was still looking to Angel for reassurance instead of her best friend.

After she gave a nod, Tate asked Ellie to scoot over so he could sit next to Nora. Ellie smiled at him. "I'll move if you give me one of your lollipops first."

Hawk snorted. "Elenora Rose!"

Ellie giggled and shrugged. "What? He has the best lollipops."

Tate chuckled and pulled a bright pink sucker from his

bag and handed it to Ellie, who then happily scooted over. Nora seemed entertained by the two of them because she was actually smiling a bit.

"Okay, let's look inside those ears," Tate said as he moved over to the couch.

Carefully, the Doc looked inside each of her ears and Angel could see he was doing his best not to touch her any more than necessary.

When he was done, Tate moved back to the coffee table across from her, his expression concerned. "Do you have any other bruises or injuries anywhere else on your body?"

She studied Tate for a second before she lifted her arm and pulled back her long sleeve, exposing a very swollen and bruised wrist. Angel took a step back and turned toward Hawk who was standing at the kitchen island a distance away. Hawk's eyes darkened and Angel was pretty sure his brother was feeling his own rage. Only, the rage Angel was feeling was ten times whatever his brother felt because Nora was *his* Little girl.

Tate examined her wrist without touching it. "Did whoever hurt you grab you by your wrist?"

Nora shook her head.

Furrowing his eyebrows, Tate looked at it again and then moved his gaze up to Nora. "Can you tell me how it got an owwie?"

Angel watched as she squeezed the small bear in her other hand before she answered Tate. "It got smashed in the car door when I was trying to run. He came after me and tried to stop me from getting in the car and slammed the door on it."

Jesus, motherfucking bastard. Raking a hand through his hair, Angel started to pace the room but a noise from Hawk made him pause. He looked up at his brother who nodded toward Nora. When he looked over at her, she looked frightened and he fucking hated that. She never had to be afraid of him. But he guessed it would take time before she realized that.

He walked over to her and knelt beside her, looking into her eyes. "Little one, if it is the last thing I do on this earth, I will make the bastard who hurt you pay dearly. No one will ever hurt you like that again. That is a promise."

She studied his face for several seconds before she slowly nodded.

Tate cleared his throat. "I want to wrap this a bit to keep her from using it too much. I think it's sprained and she's badly bruised. I won't wrap it tightly tonight since it's so swollen but if she keeps it iced tonight and doesn't use it, the swelling should be down a bit by tomorrow and then it can be wrapped a little tighter. She can also take an over-the-counter anti-inflammatory to help with the pain. I don't think anything is broken but if it doesn't start looking better in the next day or two, I'll want to x-ray it."

Angel nodded as the doc spoke to him. He hadn't actually established himself to anyone as being Nora's Daddy, but Tate must have just assumed given the way he'd threatened the doctor. Thank fuck Tate was easygoing and didn't take those threats to heart.

"I'll make sure she is all taken care of, Doc," Angel reassured him.

Tate nodded and took several minutes to wrap her wrist as gently as possible while Angel and Ellie watched. At one point, Ellie raised her gaze to Angel and gave him a knowing look. What she knew, he wasn't exactly sure.

As soon as Tate had gotten Nora taken care of, he pulled a bright orange lollipop from his bag and held it up for her. "Since you were such a good and brave girl for me."

Nora smiled, licking her lips as she reached for it with her bandaged hand. When she had the candy securely in her grip, she held out the bear to Tate, but the doctor shook his head.

"You keep him for me. I think he likes you," Tate told her softly.

Her green eyes lit up and Angel had to swallow the jealousy surging inside him at the sight of another man making his woman smile. Tate must have felt Angel glaring at him because he rose from the coffee table and grabbed his doctor's bag.

"Call me if you need anything or have any questions," Tate said to Angel before he waved to Nora and Ellie and headed for the front door with Hawk following.

Now that Nora had been looked at by a doctor, it was time to get her talking about her ex. Angel wanted to go hunting.

3

NORA

Looking over at Ellie, Nora found her best friend grinning from ear to ear as she stared up at Angel and then looked down at Nora.

"Why don't I show you to the room you'll be staying in? That way you can get settled and take a bubble bath if you want," Ellie offered.

Nora hesitated briefly before nodding. It wasn't that she didn't want to get settled and crawl into bed and maybe sleep for three or four days straight, but following Ellie to her room would take her away from Angel and for some reason, she really liked being around him. Even if she was also slightly terrified of him. The man growled a lot. And sometimes, it seemed as though his dark eyes turned black, making him look even more menacing.

Ellie stood and grabbed Nora's uninjured hand, gently pulling her up from the couch. Giving Angel one last glance, she followed Ellie out of the room, passing Hawk in the hallway as they made their way toward the stairs.

Hawk furrowed his eyebrows. "Where are you two going?"

"I'm going to show Nora her room and help her get settled," Ellie told him, lifting to her tiptoes to kiss Hawk on the lips.

Nora watched as Hawk wrapped his arm around Ellie and kissed her deeply before letting her go and giving her a swat on the bottom. Ellie giggled and stuck her tongue out at him before continuing on their mission.

Once they were upstairs, Ellie opened the door to a bedroom and when Nora walked in, she gasped. Hawk's house was huge and beautiful on both the outside and the inside. It felt welcoming and cozy and the bedroom she'd just stepped into was no exception. It was painted in a soft cream color and all the linens were white and cream shades that made the room feel clean and tranquil.

Ellie closed the door behind them and smiled at her. "You like Angel."

She could feel her eyes widen as she stared back at her friend. She didn't even know Angel. And liking anyone was not exactly something Nora excelled at. She'd only trusted two people in her entire life. One of those two people had turned into her abuser and the other person was standing right in front of her. How could she possibly like a stranger?

"No, I don't," she argued.

Rolling her eyes, Ellie walked over and sat on the edge of the bed. "You think he's cute then. You kept looking at him and you got a funny look on your face every time you guys met eyes."

Unable to stop herself from smiling, Nora rolled her eyes. "Any woman alive with working eyeballs would think he's cute but that doesn't mean I like him. He's a little scary."

Ellie shrugged. "Angel is a little scary, but he'd never hurt you or me or any of the women in the family. I don't think he would ever hurt *any* woman, for that matter. He's too protective."

Nora walked over and sat down next to her best friend, changing the subject so maybe she would stop thinking about the dark-eyed man downstairs. "I'm sorry to barge in on your life. I know you and Hawk are still new."

"It's fine. Besides, the rooms are all soundproofed in all their houses, so you won't hear if Hawk spanks my ass or makes me scream," Ellie told her with a grin.

Feeling a blush rise to her cheeks, Nora looked anywhere but at her friend.

Thankfully, Ellie changed the subject this time. "Why didn't you tell me Trevor was hurting you? How long has it been going on?"

Letting out a shallow breath, Nora could feel tears welling in her eyes. "He monitored my phone constantly, so I couldn't tell you. It would have made it worse. It was like as soon as I moved out of Seattle with him, a switch flipped and he turned into a monster. I was so isolated and scared but when he hit me, I knew I had to get out. It would have kept getting worse until he killed me."

Tears streamed down Ellie's face making Nora start to cry, too.

Ellie wrapped her arms around her. "I'm so sorry. I wish I had known. Hawk and his brothers would have come to help you in a heartbeat. You know they are going to look for him. Trevor won't get away with this."

Shaking her head, Nora released Ellie. "They can't. They just need to leave it alone. I got away from him and that's all that matters."

"What if the next person doesn't get away from him? What if he hurts another innocent woman? You wouldn't want that to happen and Daddy and his brothers sure as hell aren't going to let him get away with hurting someone in our family."

Nora wasn't sure what Ellie had meant by that since she was just Ellie's best friend. The guys had no obligation to do anything for her. But even if they wanted to, it was dangerous and she kind of already liked Hawk and Angel and that other big hairy brother and Lucy. She didn't want anything to happen to them. Maybe it had been a mistake bringing her problems into their lives but where else could she go?

You're such a loser, Nora. You can't even be strong enough to take care of yourself.

Letting out a sad sigh, she looked at Ellie. "It's too dangerous. They need to leave it alone."

A light knock on the door made her tense, and when Ellie got up to open it, Nora held her breath as she waited to see who was on the other side. Would she be scared like this for the rest of her life?

Both Hawk and Angel stood out in the hallway when Ellie opened the door. The men were holding coffee mugs and when they stepped inside, Angel offered his cup to her. "It's hot chocolate. It will soothe you."

She looked down at the cup and smiled softly. There was whipped cream on top with pink sprinkles. Definitely soothing.

"Is she ready to answer questions?" Hawk demanded.

Ellie giggled and shook her head. "Daddy, this isn't an interrogation. Calm down. She doesn't want you guys to get involved. She thinks it's too dangerous for you."

Angel and Hawk looked at each other with amused expressions and then started laughing.

"The only person who is in danger is him, Little one. You don't need to worry about us," Angel said, looking directly at Nora.

Sucking her bottom lip between her teeth, she lowered her gaze from him and stared down into her hot chocolate. "He's dangerous," she whispered.

Angel knelt in front of her. She liked when he did that. It made him seem slightly less scary. Just slightly, though. "He's not too dangerous for us. I don't know what you know about us, but we are scarier than some of the scariest monsters in the world."

She furrowed her eyebrows. What did he mean by that? She didn't know anything about them. Her conversations with Ellie had been limited to mostly text over the past few months and it had only been recently that she'd found out about her best friend moving in with Hawk.

Ellie cleared her throat. "I, uh, I haven't told her about you guys. You can trust her, though. She'd never say anything."

Raising her gaze to her best friend, Nora gave her a questioning look. The feel of a warm hand on her knee had her snapping her attention back to the person in front of her.

Angel stroked her leg with his thumb. "We protect innocent people. We find lost people. And we make the bad people pay dearly. The only thing you really need to know is that you are completely safe with us and we will protect you with our lives. So please, tell us, what's his last name, Nora?"

4

ANGEL

He waited as patiently as he could for the sweet, scared Little girl in front of him to get the courage to tell them the man's last name. Ellie didn't know anything about Trevor other than his first name and kind of what he looked like since she'd only met him briefly one time before Nora had moved out of the area with him.

Nora slowly shook her head and Angel had to fight the urge to pull her over his lap and spank the answers out of her. A spanking wasn't what she needed right then. It would be a long time before she would be ready to be spanked, especially after going through the abuse her fucker ex-boyfriend put her through.

One thing she needed to understand was just how dangerous Angel and his brothers were when it came to the ones they cared about and, even though he barely knew Nora, he cared about her. She would be fiercely protected by them, and once she understood she belonged to Angel, she would probably be ready to kill him in frustration when she found out just how overprotective he was. He would suffocate her— but it would be with good intentions.

"I'm going to let you slide without answering our questions for now, but you will answer them eventually, Little one," Angel told her.

Nora narrowed her eyes at him just briefly. It was a sign that she had some fire inside of her and even if she kept it all inside her, he could hardly wait to see those little glimpses of defiance. If she was friends with Ellie, he had no doubt that Nora could be as fierce a Little girl as her best friend. You'd have to be fierce to put up with Ellie's feistiness.

Hawk nodded. "He's right, Nora. We need to know some information so we can protect you properly. I know you're scared and you don't trust us yet, but you will eventually. We will take care of you. You're family now so you better get used to us."

Ellie snorted. "What my Daddy means is that they are cavemen and act like King Kong crashing through everything that gets in their way. Don't worry, though, Angel is one of the nicer ones. Hawk and Wolf are still learning how to live in society."

Angel laughed and noticed Nora smiling at her friend while Hawk let out a low grumbling noise.

Reaching into his pocket, Angel pulled out a phone he'd already gotten from Colt and held it out for Nora. "This is a burner phone. The only way it can be traced is by our brother, Colt. All our numbers are already programmed into it, including the Littles of the family. If you ever need anything, you call any of us guys and we will be right there, okay?"

Nora eyed the phone before reaching out and wrapping her delicate fingers around it.

"Give me your old phone so we can destroy it and make

sure he can't track you," Angel added.

Her eyes widened and she looked to Ellie, who nodded.

"Colt will make sure your old phone is untraceable and will reroute your ending location on it so if Trevor does trace your phone, he won't know you came here. You can trust them," Ellie told Nora.

Angel nodded and smiled softly at Ellie. Even though Ellie was new to the family, she fit in perfectly and accepted all the men for who they were and what they did. She was one of the first women Angel had ever met who wasn't afraid of Hawk. Ellie was brave, sweet, and kind while also being a bit of a badass Little girl. The first time Angel had watched her taking charge and bossing Hawk and him around during a dog rescue, Angel had been completely impressed by her and had known she was the perfect Little girl for his brother. What he hadn't known at the time was that Ellie would bring Nora into his life.

Nora reached behind her with her unwrapped hand and pulled her phone out of her back pocket and handed it to Angel.

"Good girl. Thank you. I'm going to get this over to Colt," he told her before turning to Ellie. "Ellie, help her make a list of everything she needs. Clothes, panties, pajamas, makeup, whatever she needs, and send it to me."

Ellie nodded. "Okay. Will do. Now, get out so we can finish gossiping."

Hawk snorted and shook his head while Angel narrowed his eyes at both women with a smirk on his face. "I can already tell you two are going to be trouble together."

Nora's lips pulled back into a soft smile, and her eyes sparkled as she looked up at him while Ellie just bobbed her head up and down.

Angel grinned and winked at Nora. "I'll talk to you later,

Little one. My number is in that phone, so if you need anything, call or text me if that's easier for you, okay?"

She nodded but didn't say anything. He had no idea how he was going to get her to open up to him, but he would learn to communicate with her somehow, even if he only got nods and head shakes as responses.

Leaving the room with Hawk, they went downstairs and stepped out onto the front porch.

Hawk eyed him. "She yours?"

Without even a single thought, Angel nodded. "Yep."

His brother grinned. "It's about time. You gonna have Colt get that fucker's phone number from her phone?"

Nodding again, Angel smiled. "Yep."

"Good. Let me know what you find out. Don't go hunting for this fucker alone, Angel. You're dangerous but you're not invincible," Hawk told him.

"For her, I'll be fucking invincible. Did you see her face? That bastard is going to die."

Angel was barely hanging onto his own rage at the moment. He hated leaving Nora. He wanted to go back into her bedroom, shut the door, pull her into his arms, and hold her forever, or at least until she felt safe and secure again.

"Yes, I fucking saw her face, and yes, he is going to die, but we know nothing about him and until we have more information, we don't go hunting. You know the biggest mistake we could make is going into a job unprepared. Be smart, Angel. All that anger and rage you keep buried, keep it fucking buried until we find him the smart way, and then you can take all of it out on him. Okay?"

He hated it when Hawk talked sensibly. Normally it was Beau or Colt or even Knox that were the more sensible ones. He was used to them being reasonable. He hated it when Hawk was being reasonable because it meant his brother was right, and that just made him want to punch the big lug.

Hawk must have been able to tell what Angel was thinking because he smirked. "You can take your anger out on me at the gym the next time we go, but you know I'm right. For now, I need to go make the girls' dinner and see if I can get Nora to say more than a word at a time to me. I need to be at least one of the Little girls' favorite uncle. Might as well win over Ellie's best friend. Keep me posted on what Colt finds out."

Nodding, Angel turned and walked away from his brother.

"Love you!" Hawk called out.

Angel turned and flipped his brother off. "Love you too, asshole."

COLT WAS SITTING on the couch with Ava on his lap when Angel let himself in. All their houses had fingerprint locks, and everyone in the family had access. Although normally, the only time any of them just walked in without knocking was when they were expected. Otherwise, who knew what someone could walk in on.

Ava had a pacifier in her mouth, and she was wrapped up in a blanket while she and Colt watched *Toy Story*.

"Hey. You get her phone?" Colt asked when he glanced at Angel coming into the living room.

Angel nodded. "Yes. She has the burner phone now."

Spitting out the pacifier, Ava grinned. "Does this mean I can send her a message now?"

Colt chuckled and shook his head. "No, Little girl. She's really shy, remember? And she's been through a lot, baby.

We need to let her ease into this family. We're a lot to take sometimes."

"Sometimes?" Ava asked.

Shooting her a stern look, Colt popped the pacifier back into her mouth and turned to Angel who was now sitting on the opposite end of the couch. "How was she?"

Angel shook his head and ran his hand over his face. "Scared to death and bruised. We had Tate come check her out to make sure she didn't have any broken bones in her face."

"Fuck," Colt murmured.

"Yeah, and she won't tell us anything about the guy so I need you to get his information off her phone. His name is Trevor."

Colt nodded. "No problem. Sit with Ava for a few and I'll go work on it now."

Nodding, Angel passed his brother the phone and leaned back against the couch, lifting his arm up. "Come on, Little girl."

Ava grinned from behind the pacifier guard and crawled over to where he was, snuggling against his side. They sat in silence watching the movie, but Angel's mind was only on Nora. He wondered about all the things he wanted to know about her. Maybe he should ask Ellie for information, but then he'd miss out on finding every single little detail about Nora in an organic way. And he didn't want to miss out on that. He wanted to see the way her eyes lit up when she would tell him something that made her happy or the way her nose crinkled when it was something she didn't like, or her tears whenever she needed to shed them. He wanted it all. The good, the bad, the ugly.

"Uncle Angel, you're thinking so loud I think I need to turn the volume up just to hear my movie," Ava said.

Looking down at her, Angel smiled and ruffled her hair. "Sorry, sweetheart."

"Are you worried about Nora?" she asked.

Not wanting to lie to her, he nodded. "I don't handle seeing abused women very well, and all I could think about when I was near her was how much I wanted to kill the guy who hurt her. She's so damn shy she wouldn't even talk to me, but I can tell she is sweet and good and didn't deserve any of what she got. No woman does."

Ava twisted her fingers in his shirt as she seemed to think about that for a few seconds. "I don't know what happened in your life, Angel, but it made you one of the most amazing men I've ever met, and I know you will make sure she never has to go through that again. I know you'll protect her with your life just like you'd do for any of us. I also know you like her, and I really hope she's the Little girl for you because you deserve your happiness."

Holy fuck. He stared down at her in shock. Ava was a sweet girl, and she was wonderful for Colt, but he hadn't spent a ton of time with her yet and this was the first time she'd ever said anything so deep to him. He'd never admit it, but he liked that the women knew he would go to war for them, because he would. He'd go to war for anyone in his family and anyone who couldn't protect themselves. Maybe if he'd gone to war as a kid, he wouldn't have seen all the things he had. The past was the past, though, as one of his therapists had told him. He couldn't change the past, but he could change the future and that's what he'd been trying to do ever since their little sister, Celeste, had been murdered.

Leaning down, he kissed the top of Ava's head. "Thanks, Little girl. I love you."

She sighed and smiled. "Love you, too, Uncle Angel. Now stop thinking so I can watch my movie."

5

NORA

Ellie had given her some clothes and pajamas to wear until she'd be able to go out and buy herself some things. Not that she really had the money for clothes. She had only a few hundred dollars in her bank account. It was the one and only thing Trevor hadn't taken over in her life. Mostly because she banked at a small, local bank that only had branches in Seattle, and once they moved, Trevor had never wanted to return to the city to get his name added to it.

Letting out a sigh, she sat on the edge of the comfy guest bed and debated on whether she wanted to actually get up and take a shower or not. Part of her wanted to get every bit of Trevor's touch washed off her skin but part of her was so tired that all she wanted to do was crawl under the covers and go to sleep.

The fact that she knew Hawk was giving Ellie a bath before putting her to bed made her feel just slightly jealous of her best friend. Of course, she was thrilled Ellie had found someone amazing, and even though Nora didn't really even know Hawk, she felt it down to her bones that he was a good man. Ellie deserved someone good. It just made Nora sad because at the moment, having a good Daddy to give her a bath and put her to bed so she didn't even have to think or worry about anything sounded like heaven.

The phone beside her vibrated, making her jump. Nora had forgotten about it since she'd always kept her cell phone on silent so Trevor wouldn't accuse her of cheating on him every time she got a call or text. Looking down at the device that Angel had given her, she immediately saw it was a text message alert and when she saw who it was from, she suddenly felt warm all over.

Why would Angel be texting her? Biting her bottom lip, she picked up the phone and used the passcode that Hawk had told her to use. Navigating to the text app, she opened the message from Angel and held her breath as she read it.

> Angel: Are you getting settled okay? Do you need anything?

Nora read the message several times. Texting was always easier for her than talking to communicate. It was probably pathetic that she struggled to talk to strangers, but texting made her feel safer. Maybe it was because the person wasn't right there in front of her and couldn't hurt her for talking or get upset because she needed a minute to figure out what she wanted to say.

Her fingers hovered over the small keyboard for several minutes before she typed back a response. Was it weird to be texting her best friend's boyfriend's brother? There was just something about Angel. It was kind of like the same feeling she had about Hawk. Both of them looked a bit terrifying but she felt deep down that they were good men. Although, she did want to ask Ellie some more questions about the earlier conversation regarding the bad stuff they did. She wished Angel would have expanded on it a bit more. Did it matter, though? Whatever they did, it seemed that they did it to help innocent people.

Staring down at her response, she hesitated to press the send button. She forced herself to take several breaths and count to three and when she got to three, she hit the little blue arrow.

> Nora: Ellie gave me some pajamas to wear and some clothes.

Within seconds, Angel replied.

> Angel: I'm glad. I'll drop off some more stuff for you tomorrow. Are you getting ready for bed?

> Nora: Not yet. I'm debating if I want to go take a quick shower before bed.

> Angel: A shower will probably make you sleep better, Little one. How about you go and take a quick shower and then get nice and cozy in bed?

She nibbled on her bottom lip. Even though he wasn't there with her, his encouragement almost made her feel as if he were taking care of her in a way. It felt good and gave her the push she needed to text him back before she got up from the bed.

> Nora: Okay

Before she made it very far, the phone vibrated again.

> Angel: Take your phone into the bathroom with you and keep it close to the shower. And text me when you get settled in bed so I know you're okay.

Her lips pulled back into a smile as she clutched the phone and carried it into the attached bathroom with her. Setting it on the counter, she started stripping her clothes off, stopping when the phone lit up again.

> Angel: If I don't hear from you in twenty minutes that you're in bed, I'm coming over there to check on you, Little one. Understand?

Giggling softly, she typed back a message. Ellie had warned her that Hawk, Angel, and the rest of the men in their family were a little over-the-top protective. She hadn't been kidding.

> Nora: Okay

> Angel: Good girl

She stared at the screen for much too long, rereading those words over and over. Those two words she'd wanted to hear so badly from her ex but had been told she didn't deserve them. And now, she was agreeing to do something so simple for her own safety and she was being called that. Good girl.

Gently unwrapping her wrist, she set the bandaging on the counter and stepped into the steaming shower. The hot water felt like heaven on her body. Even though she was sore from fighting back against Trevor, the only thing she could really focus on was how good it felt and the tingling feeling between her legs that had been there ever since Angel had walked into the house.

When was the last time she'd even felt anything down there? It had been way too long and if she were honest with herself, it had been long before she'd ever been with Trevor. That should have been a major clue.

Too tired to give in to the urge to touch herself, Nora quickly washed her body, moaning softly as she ran her soapy hands over her nipples. It felt naughty to be having such feelings and for some reason, she felt that if she touched herself, she would be doing something she shouldn't. It was silly. Why did she want permission to touch herself? Was she really that needy?

As soon as she was clean from head to toe and rinsed, she shut off the water and grabbed the towel that was hanging on the hook right outside the shower. After wrapping herself up in the fluffy terry cloth, she stepped out and walked carefully to the vanity. She was a bit wobbly, probably mostly from exhaustion. When she looked at herself in the mirror, she gasped.

Bringing her fingers up to her cheek, she winced. She hadn't realized just how purple her face was. No wonder Hawk and Angel had made her see a doctor. Shit.

Tears pooled in her eyes but she forced herself not to cry. She'd cried enough these past several months. She wasn't going to cry anymore. Not for him. He didn't deserve her tears.

By the time she'd dried herself off, gotten some pajamas on, and crawled into the bed, she realized it had almost been twenty minutes. She had no doubt if she didn't text Angel before her time was up, he would come crashing into the house like a bull in a china shop to make sure she was okay. She found it interesting that the thought of him doing that didn't scare her, but she was also a guest in Hawk and Ellie's house. No need to cause excess drama.

> Nora: I'm in bed. I'm glad I took a shower. It felt good.

Angel: Good. I'm glad. I'm sure a bath with
bubbles would have been better but
another time.

Angel: Is texting easier for you to
communicate?

Nora: Yeah. Sorry I'm so shy.

Angel: Never be sorry for that, Little one.
I'm just happy to have a way to
communicate with you that makes it easier
for you.

Angel: Did you wrap your wrist after your
shower?

Shoot. She'd forgotten. She really didn't like having her
wrist wrapped. It was itchy, so maybe she'd intentionally
forgotten.

Nora: No. It itches.

Angel: Go wrap it, Little one. Tomorrow I'll
find you a new wrap that doesn't itch but it
needs to be wrapped to heal properly.

Letting out a sigh, she got out of bed and went to the
bathroom to do as he'd said. It didn't look as well wrapped
as it had when the doctor had wrapped it but it was secure
so she called it good and climbed back into bed.

Nora: Okay. It's wrapped. I didn't do a very
good job.

Angel: That's a good girl. I'm sure you did a
fine job. As long as it has the support it
needs. I'll be over first thing in the morning
so Hawk and Ellie can go to work.

Nora: What about work for you?

Angel: My job is a little less conventional. I don't have set hours. Ellie said you edit books for work? Colt is setting up a laptop for you that I'll bring in the morning.

Nora: Thank you... for everything. You've been so nice to me.

Angel: You're safe with us, Nora. You're safe with me.

Angel: You need to rest. Sleep as long as you can and we'll talk more tomorrow. Call or text if you need anything.

Nora: Okay. Night, Angel.

Angel: Sweet dreams, Little one.

6

ANGEL

He'd slept like shit. It seemed like every few minutes he was checking his phone to see if Nora had messaged him. It was silly to even think she would in the middle of the night. If she needed anything, her best friend was in the same house as she was, so why would she reach out to him? But he really fucking wanted her to need him. It had been so long since he'd felt needed and it was a feeling he hadn't thought he wanted anymore. But he did. With Nora, he did.

Stepping into the shower, he let the water beat down on him as he lathered himself up. As he closed his eyes, Nora was the only thing he envisioned. Her wide, round hips made his cock harden and he could only wonder how amazing her breasts looked. She was probably considered plus-size but to him, she was perfect. Round and soft and beautiful. He wanted to run his hands over her creamy flesh and make her feel things she'd probably never felt before.

Fisting his cock in his hand, Angel stroked it slowly while resting his free hand on the tiled wall. Slowly moving his hand up and down his shaft, he groaned as he pictured Nora spread out in front of him while he worshipped her from head to toe. The thought of putting his mouth on her sweet little pussy was enough to make him come, shooting his seed into the spray of the water.

Maybe that would take the edge off for the time being. He was supposed to spend the day at Hawk's keeping an eye on her while his brother and Ellie went to work, and he didn't want to be walking around with a hard-on all day.

He liked that Nora was able to work remotely. With his job, he could work from anywhere except for the times he had to travel, something he would be changing in the near future. His clients could start coming to him more. Once Nora was his, he was going to be home with her as often as possible.

Once dressed in a pair of jeans, a soft T-shirt, and a pair of boots, he grabbed his own laptop and the laptop Colt had set up for her as well as the bags of clothes and hygiene products he'd bought for Nora, and walked three houses down the street to Hawk's, letting himself in with his finger-print. They were expecting him but apparently that didn't matter because when he walked into the kitchen, Ellie was bent over one of the bar stools while Hawk gave her several hard swats over her scrub pants.

Ellie whimpered and wiggled but it was obvious she wasn't hating it completely.

When Hawk stopped, he kept a hand on her lower back so she couldn't rise. "If I have to remind you to eat breakfast before work again, the next conversation will be with your bottom bared and the hairbrush in my hand. Are we clear?"

She sniffed. "Yes, Daddy."

Hawk nodded and let her up from the stool. "Morning, Angel."

Ellie spun around, meeting Angel's gaze. Her cheeks

were as red as ripe tomatoes. It wasn't the first time he'd seen the Littles in the family get spanked. It was actually pretty common. Though, this was the first time he'd seen Ellie getting corrected like that. She lowered her gaze from his then glanced up at Hawk, who wasn't even facing Angel.

"How did you know he was here?" she asked Hawk.

Cupping her chin, Hawk kissed the tip of her nose. "I know everything that happens in this house, Little girl. Which would be good for you to remember because that little candy stash you had hidden behind the books in the den is long gone."

Angel chuckled as Ellie's mouth dropped open and she stared up at Hawk like he'd given her the worst news in the world.

"That's so mean, Daddy," she mumbled.

Shaking his head, Hawk walked over to the coffee pot and poured Angel a cup. "We haven't seen Nora yet this morning."

Angel reached out and took the steaming hot mug of coffee from his brother and nodded. "I told her to sleep as long as she could."

Ellie furrowed her eyebrows as she looked at Angel. "When did you talk to her?"

"Last night. I texted her to check on her before bed. She's a little more talkative over text," Angel told them.

He could see the corners of Ellie's lips turning up into a smile. It wouldn't be long before every Little in the family knew he liked Nora. Hell, they probably already knew considering how fast news seemed to travel between them in their group text chat.

Hawk shot Ellie a look. "Mind your business, Little girl. Let them figure it out."

Ellie's bottom lip popped out in a pout, but she nodded.

Angel winked at her. "Don't worry, Ellie. I'll take good care of her."

She grinned. "I know you will. My Daddy will kill you if you don't."

Hawk snorted. "Signing me up for jobs, huh, brat?"

"Yep," she replied, flashing Hawk an innocent smile.

"Go brush your teeth and then we'll go," Hawk told her as he picked up her pink plastic plate from the kitchen island and put it in the sink.

As soon as she disappeared, Hawk looked at Angel. "Hear anything from Colt?"

Shaking his head, Angel leaned against the counter. "Not yet. He got her phone retracked last night. Now he's trying to find information on the fucker based on the number she had for him in her phone. Did Nora eat dinner last night?"

"Barely. She did thank me for dinner and said goodnight to me, so I think that's progress," Hawk said, shrugging his shoulders.

Yeah, it was progress. He just wished he knew why she was so shy. Had something happened to her in her past? She was terrified of doctors, but a lot of Littles were. It wasn't totally unusual. He'd never met someone quite so shy and quiet and it made him wonder if it was something more. Something deeper. It would take time but he would find out sooner or later, and he would do whatever it took to help her heal.

After Hawk and Ellie left for work, Angel sat down on the couch and opened his laptop, waiting for Nora to wake up. He spent the next hour answering emails.

When he heard the soft pitter-patter of feet coming down the stairs, he held his breath as he waited for Nora to appear in the living room. He wasn't prepared for the sight he saw, though. Even though her cheek was still terribly bruised, she looked adorable. Her dark brown hair was a wild mess from sleeping. The pajamas Ellie had given her had teddy bears printed all over the pants and matching top, and she looked like she'd only woken up about three seconds before coming down the stairs.

Her gaze locked with his and she stopped mid-step and gave him a small wave with her uninjured hand.

"Morning, Little one. Did you sleep well?"

She nodded and looked around the room as if searching for Ellie or Hawk.

Angel stood and walked into the kitchen, making sure to give her space as he went past her. "Hawk and Ellie already went to work. Do you want some juice or coffee?"

Tucking a piece of hair behind her ear, she walked toward the kitchen. "Coffee, please?" she said quietly.

Nodding, he poured her a cup and grabbed the sweet-flavored creamer that Ellie used out of the fridge and held it up for her. She nodded and smiled.

"Sit down and relax, Little one. I'll bring it to you. Are you hungry or do you need a few minutes to wake up before you eat?"

Asking her questions she couldn't shake her head or nod to answer was intentional. He wanted her to get used to talking to him and hoped that even if they were short answers it would help.

"Not hungry," she murmured as she went and sat on the couch.

He followed her and set the cup of coffee on the table in front of her, then sat down at the opposite end, giving her some space. He was glad she wasn't trembling like she had been the night before.

Picking up the remote, he flipped to a cartoon channel and sat back, taking a drink of his own coffee as they watched TV. He wasn't sure how to break the ice in person with her. Over text seemed to be easier for her but it would be silly to text her from the other side of the couch.

Finally, after rolling around different ideas in his head, he turned to her. "What do you call a pile of cats?"

She looked at him with the cutest confused expression.

"A meow-ntain," he told her.

A slow smile spread across her face and when she let out the smallest of giggles, he felt like a goddamn king.

He grinned and winked at her. "I have more where that came from."

She giggled again and rolled her eyes. "You're silly."

"I'll be silly all day long if it means I get to see your sweet smile and those cute little dimples."

Her cheeks turned pink as she lowered her gaze from his.

"Look at me, Nora."

When she obeyed and met his eyes again, he was pleased. "Don't ever be afraid to look me in the eye, Little one. I'll never hurt you."

Her expression turned sad as she nibbled on her bottom lip.

"That's what he said, too," she finally whispered.

Yeah. That didn't surprise Angel. So many abusers were too fucking smooth in the beginning before turning into monsters. And while Angel might be a monster to the people who deserved to see that side of him, she would only see the caring and protective side of him. "The difference is I'm telling the truth. You can ask anyone in my family. In fact, I would encourage you to talk to them. The Littles will tell you everything about me, even the embarrassing stuff. But they'll also tell you I would never hurt you or any of them. Just like Hawk, I'm a Daddy. I'm not a fake Daddy like the asshole who hurt you."

Her eyes widened. "You know I'm Little?"

Smiling softly, he nodded. "Yeah, baby girl. I know. It's pretty obvious, and Ellie might have slipped up and mentioned the guy you were with was supposed to be a Daddy Dom."

Staring down at her hands, she picked at her cuticles and Angel could see tears pooling in her eyes.

"Nora."

When she lifted her gaze to him, her tears spilled down her cheeks and he couldn't stop himself from moving closer to her. "Baby girl, I want to hold you, but I don't want to do anything that will make you uncomfortable. I'm not going to touch you, but I want you to know that any time you need to be hugged, held, comforted, reassured, coddled, or anything at all, you can come to me. I feel this over-whelming need to take care of you, but I also know you're scared of me so I'm going to try to move as slow as I can with you, okay?"

Wiping away her tears with the backs of her hands, she shook her head. "I'm too much trouble," she whispered.

He resisted the urge to reach out and cup her chin so she was forced to keep her gaze on him. He wanted to see those beautiful green eyes as she absorbed everything he had to say to her. "You're not too much trouble. Not for the right Daddy. Not for the right man. We'll work on you remembering that because I don't like you thinking of your-self that way."

When she didn't reply, he sat back against the couch again, though he was only about a foot away from her this time, and continued watching the show that was on.

They spent the rest of the day like this. Angel got a few calls here and there and for the most part he let them go to voicemail. But when Colt called, he went into Hawk's office and closed the door behind him.

"What do you have for me?"

"I wish I had something but the phone number she had programmed into her phone attached to his name is a burner phone. It's not attached to anyone. It's a ghost cell."

Fuck. That wasn't what he wanted to hear. Why the fuck would someone have a burner phone unless they had a reason for needing it? An average, everyday person didn't just walk around with one of those. Angel and his brothers used them regularly for jobs and whenever there was a situation where someone needed to be untraceable, like Nora at the moment. There was something more to this guy and he really needed Nora to cooperate. Maybe she'd be more willing while they were one on one instead of with Hawk and Ellie there.

"Can you keep digging into her phone to try to find something? I'm here with her now and I'm going to try to get information."

"For sure. I'll call you if I find anything."

Angel hung up the call and sighed. Now, he had to try and get his Little girl to talk. He had a feeling even in an interrogation she wouldn't crack so he didn't know if he would have any luck, but he would sure as hell try because each passing minute this fucker was alive just made the rage fire burn even hotter inside of him.

7

NORA

She kept looking down the hall toward the office door Angel had shut behind him. As soon as she'd heard the latch click into place, she'd felt a sense of loss. Even though their conversations through the day had been short and limited, his presence alone had made her feel safe and, most of all, Little. She couldn't remember the last time she'd felt those two things at the same time.

Angel had made her breakfast and lunch and both times, he'd given her meals to her on cute little plastic plates. The sandwich he'd made her for lunch was cut into triangles with the crust cut off, too. It was sweet and thoughtful and made her have to swallow down the lump that had formed in her throat each time. Even in the beginning of her relationship with Trevor, he had never been that attentive. He'd expected her to make meals for him, not the other way around. That probably should have been another red flag right there.

When the office door opened, she forced herself to keep her gaze on the TV as he came back into the living room and sat next to her again. Ever since he'd moved closer to her that morning, he always sat back down next to her, close enough she could smell the citrus cologne he wore. She'd also memorized all the symbols tattooed on his fingers so she could look them up later to find out what they meant.

"Baby girl, we need to talk. I really need your help with answering some questions for me."

Her entire body tensed. She knew Hawk, Angel, and the rest of their brothers weren't going to stop until they had the answers they wanted. Ellie had warned her the night before that whether Nora liked it or not, the men would find Trevor and take care of him. Whatever that meant. It sounded like they were going to kill him, but people didn't just go around killing bad people. That was stuff that only happened in the movies. Not in real life.

"What is Trevor's last name?" Angel asked.

Picking at the pajamas she was still wearing, she raised her gaze to his. "Why do you need to know?"

Angel leaned forward, resting his elbows on his knees as he looked over at her. "Because his phone number in your phone is a ghost phone, meaning it isn't attached to him. People only use ghost phones if they are trying to hide something. What is he hiding, Nora?"

Shrugging, she pulled her bottom lip between her teeth and sighed. "I don't know. He would always fly off the handle when I asked questions. He always told me to stop getting into his business and just do what I'm told."

Like a switch, Angel's eyes darkened to black as he clenched his fists. "Baby girl, never, ever, be afraid to ask me anything. You want to know my bank account number, you ask and I will hand it over. Understand me? I will never hide anything from you. You're mine, Nora. Maybe not officially but one day you will be. I can feel it deep down inside of me so I want you to know that even if you're not officially mine yet, my business is your business. Understand?"

Wow. Angel was... intense. She probably should have been running for the hills, but she didn't want to run that way. She wanted to run toward him. Although, she wasn't so sure about the whole "she was his" thing. The last thing she needed was someone else taking over her life the way Trevor had. She was so damaged just from that one relationship plus the damage from her childhood. Now, she was too fucked up inside to handle another relationship.

Not to mention her problems would quickly grow old with Angel just like they had with Trevor and then she'd no longer be wanted. It was just better to keep her distance. As soon as she got her next paycheck, she would leave Seattle and head somewhere else. Somewhere Trevor would never find her and she could live a life in seclusion. It would be better for everyone.

It would be a sad and lonely existence for her but besides Ellie, no one had ever made her feel worthy of even living so it was probably for the best.

"Nora, baby, tell me you understand what I just said."

Slowly raising her gaze to Angel's, she gave him a slight nod. She had a feeling he wouldn't give up until she told him she understood. Besides, she could understand what he said perfectly. The reality of what he said just didn't seem real, though.

"Please tell me his last name, baby girl."

It was inevitable that they would find out. All of them seemed to be like a dog going after a meaty bone. They wouldn't stop until they were satisfied. Which was kind of endearing in a way because it was obvious they wanted to get revenge for her, and that was pretty sweet considering she'd never met any of these people before.

She let out a deep sigh. "It's Thomas."

Angel nodded. "Good girl. Thank you. I need to send Colt a text. Do you want to find another movie for us to watch?"

Reaching out, she put her hand on his wrist to stop him from sending the text to his brother. He looked up at her in surprise.

"Angel, he's a cop. More specifically a detective. He's well respected and has the entire police force in his pocket. He's dangerous."

Putting his other hand on top of hers, Angel squeezed it gently. "Not as dangerous as I am when someone messes with what's mine."

It felt as though the wind had been knocked out of her. All his declarations of her being his should have her calling the police, not wanting to crawl into his lap and hide there forever.

When he released her hand, he sent a text then sat back on the couch like she hadn't just told him something huge and nodded toward the TV. "What movie are we watching next, Little one?"

"So how was your day with Angel?" Ellie asked.

The women were up in the guest bedroom, putting away the bags and bags of clothes that Angel had picked up for her. She'd never be able to pay him back for everything he'd gotten her.

Running her hands over the softest cotton dress she'd ever felt, Nora smiled. "Awkward but good. He wasn't awkward. Just me. As usual."

Ellie stopped what she was doing by the dresser, walked over to where Nora was sitting on the bed, and wrapped her arm around her. "You're not awkward, Nora.

You're perfect just the way you are. You always have been."

Leaning her head down on Ellie's shoulder, Nora sighed. "I just wish I could be normal like you. You can talk to anyone with no problem."

"I might be able to talk to anyone with no problem but you, my sweet friend, can keep a secret better than anyone I've ever known. And you do so many other things way better than me. Everyone has different things they're good at. Besides, you kept your mouth shut so you would survive your father. That trauma doesn't just go away overnight. Sometimes never. The important thing is finding the people you can trust and working to open up with them. I promise you can trust Angel."

Nora hugged a pillow to her chest. "How do you know I can trust him?"

"Because Hawk and the rest of his brothers wouldn't allow a bad person to be a part of the family. I'm not saying Angel doesn't have issues. He does. They all do. I don't want to tell his story but what I will say is that Leo is the head of the family and Beau is the only biological kid of Leo's. The rest of the guys were brought into the family in their teens after they'd been through some horrific shit in their lives. Some of them have been to jail, some of them sold drugs, some of them were terribly abused by their families and ran away. I don't know Angel's story. All I know is Hawk told me he had the darkest background.

"Angel can be intense, and the one time I saw his mean side come out, it wasn't pretty, but it was when they were saving me from my old boss. You should talk to Addie and Kylie. They've been in the family the longest of all the Littles," Ellie said.

It made her sad to think that Angel had a hard background. She wondered about the things that had happened in his life to make him so strong and protective. She also wondered what he'd meant by the bad stuff they do for the greater good and now was the perfect time to ask Ellie. "Tell me what you meant when you said they do bad stuff?"

Ellie stood from the bed and went back to putting clothes in the dresser. "I'm telling you because I know you would never tell a soul. I also asked Hawk if I could tell you and he said I could.

"Hawk and Angel and the rest of them are like vigilantes. They help innocent people. They hurt bad people. Celeste, their younger sister, was murdered when she was nineteen by a gang because Leo wouldn't give the gang his fighting circuit. After she was murdered, Angel and the rest of them wiped out the entire gang one by one to avenge Celeste.

"Ever since then, they have been taking jobs. They saved Dr. Tate's daughter when she was kidnapped. They saved Addie after her ex-boyfriend kidnapped her. There's a lot to it but they only hurt people who hurt other people."

Nora was pretty sure her mouth was hanging open. That was a lot of information. Not just regular information, either. How was she supposed to react to that? What they did sounded like a good thing. It sounded like they helped a lot of people and did things the police weren't able to do. But... "Do they kill people?" she asked quietly as if they could be overheard.

Her best friend walked over and sat beside her again, taking her uninjured hand in both of hers. "They do what they have to do to remove the threats in the world. Sometimes people die. Sometimes at their hands and sometimes at the hands of the people who hired them. Either way, they help get rid of sex predators, human traffickers, kidnappers, abusers, and anyone else who hurts innocent women and children."

That was a lot to absorb. Did it change her opinion on Hawk or Angel? It didn't feel like it did. In fact, in a way, it made her feel safer.

"They never get caught?" she asked.

Ellie shook her head. "The people who hire them are rich as fuck usually and provide every single thing they need to do the job without getting caught. They're well trained and they have a lot of help. And if they were to ever get caught, they have safeguards in place for all us women so we're taken care of for life."

Holy shit. These guys were something else. Heroes? Yeah, she would consider them that. Who would risk their own lives to save people? It was admirable. If only she'd had people like that come into her life when she was a kid, maybe she wouldn't be as fucked up as she was now. It still scared her, though. She barely knew Angel, but she already knew she would be sad if anything ever happened to him.

And what does that mean? That you like him a lot more than you realize.

8

ANGEL

H̲e hated leaving Nora, but he had some calls he needed to make and Angel knew she was in good hands with Hawk.

It took nearly two hours to make all his calls and rearrange his work schedule. The nice thing about being self-employed was being able to call the shots and if his clients wanted his help, they could come to him from now on.

Just as he was pulling a beer from the fridge, his phone chimed with a text message. Pulling the device from his back pocket, he saw Ellie's name on the screen.

Ellie: She knows about the shadows.

Fuck. That could be bad.

Angel: How did she react?

Ellie: Just as I suspected.

What the fuck. That told him nothing. Pressing the call

button, he waited until Ellie picked up. She answered, giggling into the phone.

"Little girl, start talking before I call Hawk and tell him to spank your ass," he growled.

"Uncle Angel, I thought you were the nicest uncle but I'm really starting to think it's Colt. You've been tattling on us a lot lately," Ellie sassed.

Good god, give him the strength. These Littles could be so damn sweet and cute but they could also be such brats and, while he'd normally indulge them, this was not one of those times. "Ellie," he ground out.

She let out a dramatic sigh. "Finnnne. She took it well. I don't know for sure, but I'll bet she was thinking she wished she'd had one of you guys to save her during her childhood."

Furrowing his eyebrows, his grip tightened on his phone. "What happened to her, Ellie? Give me names."

"You need to ask her those questions, Angel."

Letting out a frustrated sigh, he looked up at the ceiling and counted to ten. "She will hardly talk to me. I doubt she's going to tell me her life story if I ask her."

"Well, that kind of sounds like a you problem, Uncle Angel. Maybe you need to have a little patience and let her open up to you when she's ready."

He really, really, wanted to spank Ellie's ass. On one hand, he respected that she didn't want to divulge her best friend's past but on the other, he wanted to make every single person who ever hurt Nora disappear from the planet. "You're really being a mean Little girl right now, Elenora Rose."

Ellie giggled. "I'm sorry, Angel. I'm not trying to be. You know I love you and I spoke very highly of you to her. I think she likes you, she's just terrified of people. Men especially. Trevor is the only man she ever opened up to and dated and he hurt her so I'm sure she's even more scared now. You're going to have to move at her pace, even if you don't like it."

Letting out a grunt, he sighed. "I don't like it when you're right."

"I know. Daddy doesn't like it, either. It happens a lot, though, so he's getting used to it."

He rolled his eyes. She really fit in a little too well with the other Littles. "Love you, brat."

"Love you, too! Bye!"

IT WAS TAKING extreme restraint not to spend all his time over at Hawk's house just so he could be close to Nora. It didn't even matter if she talked to him or not, he just wanted to be around her so he could watch over her, take care of her, and make sure she had everything she could ever want or need.

He worried about her bandaged wrist. Was it healing? It had looked okay earlier in the day when he helped her re-wrap it with a different, hopefully less itchy wrap, but he wanted to check again. He wanted to make sure she was taking her pain medicine and that she was drinking enough water.

Instead of going to Hawk's, he opted to go to Colt's to see if his brother had any information based on that fucker's last name and the fact that he was a cop. Angel didn't give a shit if he was the goddamn sheriff. The guy was an abuser and chances were, Nora wasn't his first victim. And if they didn't find him soon, it was possible she wouldn't be his last, either.

Ava and Addie were both wearing tutus and dancing in the middle of the living room when he walked into Colt's house that evening. It looked like they were playing some game but whatever it was they were doing, they looked adorable.

"Hey, bro," Knox greeted from where he sat at the kitchen island that was open to the living room.

Colt nodded to Angel and reached into the fridge, pulling out a beer.

Angel took the cold bottle from his brother and opened it before taking a long drink. "What's new?"

Knox and Colt exchanged glances before they both looked at him.

"What?" Angel asked.

Colt looked hesitant to speak.

"You said the guy's name was Trevor Thomas?" Knox asked.

Nodding, Angel looked at each of his brothers. "Yeah. Why?"

"Trevor Thomas. Does that name ring a bell at all?" Colt asked.

It sounded familiar but it was also a common name, so Angel hadn't really thought about it. "Did you find out who he is?"

"He's an actor who played a detective role in a TV series in the sixties... who died years ago," Knox told him.

What?

"I looked in the police database for all of Washington and Oregon and there is no Trevor Thomas in any of the precincts and there hasn't been for the last ten years," Colt replied.

Angel's blood ran cold. It wasn't a real name. Who was this sick fuck?

"He gave her a fake name. Unless she's not telling us the truth. But at this point, we have no idea who this guy is or if he is even a cop," Knox said.

Shaking his head, Angel stared out at the living room, watching the Little girls dance and giggle to the music playing on the game. "I can't believe this. I don't think she's lying. I think she got lied to. Fuck. This guy preyed on her."

Colt took a swig of his beer and nodded. "Try to get some more information from her. Where did they live? What kind of car does he drive? Does she remember any part of his license plate?"

Yeah... Angel was pretty sure it would be easier to get that information from a cat in heat before he got it from her. He needed to be patient, and for her, he would be, but it was hard because he wanted to get revenge on the guy who hurt her. And whoever had hurt her in the past.

Scrubbing a hand over his face, Angel nodded. "I'll see what I can do. Thanks for checking."

Angel: What did you eat for dinner?

Nora: Hawk made spaghetti.

Angel: What's your favorite dinner ever?

Nora: Macaroni and cheese.

Angel: LOL. I don't know if macaroni and cheese counts as a full meal.

Nora: Of course it does.

ANGEL FOUND himself grinning down at his phone as he typed another message.

Angel: Are you ready for bed, baby girl?

Nora: Getting there. Taking a bath now.

Fuck. She was texting him from the tub. He wanted to be there to bathe her. To wash every crevice and curve of her body then dry her off and feast on her for a while before putting her into some soft pajamas that made her feel Little.

Ignoring his cock pressing painfully against the fly of his jeans, he typed back a message.

Angel: Text me when you're settled in bed.

While waiting for her to text him, he sent a text to Hawk explaining what he'd found out from Knox and Colt. The guy they were searching for was obviously some kind of psycho. Was he really even a cop or did he tell Nora that to frighten her or even possibly to make her feel safe in the beginning? Most people think of cops as being safe people. And they should be. That was the whole point of having police officers in the world. To make people feel safe.

His phone chimed and he saw Nora's name. She was already such a good girl. Angel was pretty sure she wasn't the bratting type. At least not yet. Maybe once she knew she was safe to be.

Nora: I'm in bed.

Angel: Good girl. What's your favorite animal?

Nora: Hippos.

Angels: Hippos are fun.

Nora: Ellie told me some stuff about you today.

Fuck. He didn't want to explain himself over text. Hitting the call button, he hoped she'd answer. It only took two rings before she did.

"Hello?" she answered softly.

"Baby girl, I want to explain a little more in detail. I don't know what Ellie told you, but I want to answer any questions you might have. I don't want you to be afraid of me."

"I'm not afraid of you," she said softly. "I mean, not any more than I'm afraid of anyone else."

Letting out a slow exhale, he felt his heart squeeze in his chest. "You should never have to be afraid of people in your life, Nora. I would never hurt you, Little one. Never, ever. I'd put a bullet in my head before I'd allow that ever to happen."

"I know. Ellie told me I can trust you. All of you."

He nodded even though she couldn't see him. He needed to hug Ellie the next time he saw her. "You can trust us, Little one. I know, though, when you've been through a lot of scary stuff that trust doesn't come easily. I'll earn your trust, though. All of us will."

When she didn't say anything, he continued. "Do you have any questions about the work we do?"

It took her several seconds before she spoke, and he was pretty sure he held his breath until she did.

"You only hurt bad people?" she asked.

"Only bad people, baby. We never want to hurt anyone unless it's absolutely necessary. Our main goal is to save people or avenge the people who have been hurt by predators. We never hurt women or children. All of us have seen women we cared about be abused or worse at some point in our lives and most of us were abused as kids. We want to do everything we can to stop that from happening to other women and kids."

"That's all I needed to know. I think what you guys do is good."

"Okay, Little one. Don't ever hesitate to ask me questions if you have them. I won't tell you specific details because I don't want to put that burden on you, but I will always answer your questions honestly."

"Thank you."

"You're welcome. Are you getting sleepy?"

He heard a soft sigh through the phone and he ached to be there with her, tucking her in.

"Kind of."

"Okay. You should close your eyes and sleep, then. I'm a call or text away, okay?"

"'Kay. Angel..."

"Yeah, baby girl?"

"I know you're going to go after Trevor no matter what. Just be careful, okay? I... I'd be sad if you got hurt."

Hooooly fuck. She'd just pulled at every heartstring he had. The fact that she'd be sad if he got hurt meant that whether she realized it or not, she felt something for him, too, and even if it was small, it was progress.

"I promise, baby girl. I'm not going anywhere."

She let out a soft giggle. "I can kind of tell."

Chuckling, Angel felt on top of the world. This had been the most he'd heard her voice and it was such a sweet sound. He'd never get tired of hearing it and knew getting to hear her talk was a very special gift.

"See you in the morning, Little one."

"Night, Angel."

9

NORA

Before she wandered downstairs the next morning, Nora had taken a moment to freshen up her hair and brush her teeth in the bathroom. Angel always looked mouthwatering, and she was pretty sure she looked like a bruised sack of potatoes in comparison. She didn't know why the man seemed to like her so much, but he was making it pretty obvious that he did. And she definitely hadn't stopped thinking about him since they'd first met.

Angel was already downstairs on the couch when she walked into the living room. He had a laptop in front of him, but as soon as she came into the room, he closed it and turned to her, smiling.

"Morning, Little one."

Everything in her body automatically wanted to shy away but at the same time, she didn't want to. She'd enjoyed talking to him on the phone the night before and had found it easier to do since they weren't face to face.

Be brave, Nora. You can trust him. He won't hurt you.

"Morning," she murmured as she made her way into the kitchen to get a cup of coffee.

Angel met her there and grabbed a coffee cup before she was able to do it herself. She watched as he poured the steaming hot coffee into the mug, glancing over at her with one of those sexy smiles that made her panties dampen. When he broke their gaze, he went and grabbed the creamer from the fridge and poured the perfect amount into her cup before handing it to her.

"Blow on it, baby girl. I don't want you to burn your mouth."

She stared at him with wide eyes. Was he really worrying about her burning her mouth on coffee? Ellie had mentioned the men were overprotective. Apparently, her friend wasn't fibbing.

Slowly, she took a drink and hummed in appreciation. It was perfect. "Did I interrupt you working?"

He shook his head. "No matter what I'm doing, when it comes to you, it's a welcome interruption."

A blush rose to her cheeks as he studied her with his dark eyes. There was hunger in those eyes, hunger for her, and that made her feel warm. She felt heat rise to her face. The tingling between her legs spread through her belly and down along her thighs. It was such a foreign but delicious feeling. She needed to ignore it, though, and find something to talk about to get her mind off the sexy man towering over her.

"What do you do for work?" she finally asked.

Leaning his hip against the counter, he crossed his muscular arms over his chest. Her knees went weak as she stared at him. Not only was he totally ripped but he was tattooed all down his arms and on the backs of his hands, making him look so incredibly intense. His piercing eyes seemed to drill into her soul. It felt intimate.

"I work for myself. I coach professional fighters on how to fight to win. I analyze fights and figure out fighters' weaknesses, then teach my clients how to use those weaknesses to win."

Whoa. That seemed big. Professional fighters? Like celebrities?

"Do you fight, too?" she asked quietly.

Ellie had mentioned that one of the brothers owned an MMA gym.

Angel nodded. "Only for exercise these days and to let out a little aggression on my brothers when they piss me off."

She wasn't sure what he meant by "these days". It sounded as if he used to fight for more than just exercise but she wasn't feeling brave enough to ask. Asking questions had gotten her screamed at by her ex for being too nosy.

"Look at me, Nora," Angel said softly.

She slowly raised her gaze to his.

"I can tell you have some sort of question floating around in that pretty little head of yours. What did I tell you about asking me questions?"

Letting out a soft sigh, she held the cup of coffee between her hands, using the warmth to help soothe her. "You said I could always ask you anything."

He nodded. "And I meant it, Little one. I will never get angry with you for asking questions. So tell me what you want to know."

"I was just wondering if you used to fight professionally?"

"I wasn't a professional, but I used to fight as a job. Pop, our dad, you'll meet him soon, owned an illegal fighting circuit. He wouldn't allow us to fight when we were underage but as soon as I turned eighteen, I talked him into letting me fight. I needed an outlet for my anger. I struggled a lot as a kid and Pop knew it. I fought in the circuit for seven years before I gave it up to do what I'm doing now."

She was pretty sure her eyes were as big as saucers. "Wow. You must have been really good."

Smiling, Angel took a step closer to her, lowering his arms to his sides. "I was good and it was good therapy for the darkness inside me at the time. But the circuit is much more dangerous than professional fighting and I didn't want to get hurt or killed. Now my therapy is kicking Hawk's ass in the ring."

That thought made her giggle. Hawk was a big guy but so was Angel.

"Go sit, Little one. I'm going to make you some breakfast. Then we have movies to watch, and it's my turn to ask some questions."

Oh great. She was afraid of that.

"Why do cows wear bells?"

Looking over at Angel out of the corner of her eye, she couldn't stop the grin that spread across her face. Apparently, his form of questions was silly jokes but with each joke he told, she felt herself relaxing a tiny bit more. It was endearing that this big, tattooed, ex-fighter of a guy spent time telling her jokes.

Thinking about the question, she scrunched up her nose. "I have no idea."

When she looked over at him, he winked and grinned, showing off his brilliant white teeth. "Because their horns don't work."

She broke out into giggles, shaking her head. "You're silly."

Leaning his head back on the couch, he looked over at her, his expression turning serious. "Life is too short not to have fun and be silly."

What he said made her feel a little bit sad inside. There was nothing happy or laughable in her home life and as a child, the only time she could remember being silly or having fun was when she was hanging out with Ellie. Now there were so many things to look forward to. She needed to learn to have some fun. One day, maybe. If she could ever stop being so damn afraid of everything.

"What do you like to do for fun when you're in Little Space?" he asked.

At first, she felt herself tense, unsure if she wanted to answer for fear of being ridiculed. Then she reminded herself who she was talking to, and it only took one look at him to realize he seemed genuinely curious. But was talking about her Little with a man she barely knew okay?

With Trevor, they had talked online for months before they'd ever met in person and during the first few months, they hadn't talked about any of that kind of stuff. She'd thought that had been a good sign, that he hadn't just been asking her questions about her Little side and her kinks. Maybe getting things out in the open was a good thing. And maybe she'd be able to learn about his Daddy side. If anything, she'd be able to fantasize about him as her Daddy while she touched herself.

"I like watching movies. I also like coloring. I like toys and games, too," she answered quietly.

Angel nodded. "Sounds like the other Littles in the family. What's your favorite toy?"

She could feel herself blushing as a slow smile spread. "I like baby dolls the most. Ellie and I always played dolls together before I moved away."

"Baby dolls, huh? We'll need to get you some of those."

The idea of having a new baby doll made her excited.

Angel got up and walked over to the hall closet, opening it up. When he closed the door and started walking back toward her, she noticed a purple stuffed toy in his hand. He brought it over to her and held it out. "Until we can get you some dolls, I hope this will give you some comfort and make you feel Little."

Her eyes Filled with tears as she reached for the purple hippo stuffie. It was big enough to hug and the fur was so soft and velvety that she couldn't stop herself from rubbing it on her cheek. She quickly wiped her eyes and looked up at him. "Thank you."

This time when he sat, he sat right next to her. "You're welcome, sweet girl. I'm sorry you had to leave your toys behind. We'll get you lots of new ones, okay?"

The lump in her throat was too big for her to talk so she just nodded and hugged the toy again before leaning over against Angel's side. It wasn't something she'd thought about before she did it, and she even surprised herself a little, but as soon as he wrapped his arm around her, she instantly felt so safe and Little. Probably the most she'd ever felt in her life and that knowledge rocked her to the core. He might be practically a stranger but it didn't matter because somehow, it felt like they'd known each other forever.

SHIFTING, her eyes fluttered open and Nora realized she had fallen asleep against Angel. Moving her head to look up at him, she realized she'd lodged her thumb in her mouth at some point. Quickly pulling it free, she raised her gaze to find him looking down at her with a gentle look on his face.

"Hey, sleepyhead," he murmured.

The purple hippo was still in her arms, and she felt so comfortable she didn't want to move, but her bladder totally disagreed with her. She moved quickly to get up and hurried to the bathroom before she had an accident. Thankfully, she made it just in time and when she finished, she washed her hands before leaving the bathroom. To her surprise, she found Angel standing close by, leaning on the opposite wall.

"I just wanted to be near in case you needed help," he told her.

Help? What would she need help with? Then again, she knew Hawk diapered Ellie and helped her use the toilet frequently so maybe that was the type of Daddy Angel was, too.

Being taken care of in such intimate and sometimes embarrassing ways was something Nora had always read and fantasized about before she'd met Trevor, and in the beginning, he even did those things. He kept her diapered often, and it had become such a comfort for her. It instantly put her in a Little headspace.

When things started getting bad, he'd started neglecting to change her so she was getting rashes but, when she told him she would just wear panties and use the toilet, he'd gotten angry and accused her of making him feel like a bad Daddy. If only she'd realized then that something was off.

She missed wearing diapers. She also missed feeling Little. It had been a long time since she'd been able to relax and feel safe enough for that. Being around Angel made her feel Little, though, and he wasn't even Daddying her. Well, not really. He sort of was. The man had come and stood outside of the bathroom after all.

"Thank you. I just really had to go," she murmured, looking everywhere but at him.

"Okay, baby girl. Come on, let's make you some lunch."

THEY SPENT THE AFTERNOON WORKING. She needed to get caught up on work so they turned on soothing music and sat on the couch with their laptops. It was comfortable but at the same time distracting. Angel made her take several breaks to ice her wrist, though. It was so sweet how he fussed over her.

The longer they worked, the more the scent of him surrounded her and made her feel all tingly and whenever she looked over at him, her breathing turned rapid. She'd never been so aroused in her life. Her panties were uncomfortably wet.

After a couple of hours, Angel set his laptop on the coffee table before reaching over and moving hers there as well. He gently grabbed hold of her hand. "You need to take a break and have a nap. You're still healing."

A nap did sound nice, but it also meant she would be away from him and she was really growing to like being around him.

"I want to tuck you in for your nap but only if you feel comfortable with that. I promise to be the perfect gentleman. Do you trust me, Little one?"

That was a loaded question. Trust was a funny thing. She barely knew Angel, yet she trusted him. It didn't mean she wasn't afraid, because she was. She was petrified. But not of him. She was afraid that her heart would get broken and somehow, she knew being hurt by Angel would be more painful than the hurt she'd experienced from both her father and from Trevor.

"I trust you."

Nodding, he stood and leaned over, scooping her up from the couch. Slipping her arm around his neck, she rested her head on his chest as he carried her through the house and up the stairs until they were in the guest bedroom where he set her carefully down on the bed.

"Crawl under the covers, baby girl. I'm going to go see if I can find a story to read you. I'll be right back."

She watched him disappear out of the room before she crawled up to the pillows and wiggled down under the covers. When Angel returned a few minutes later, he had a picture book in one hand and the stuffed hippo in another.

Yeah, her heart was definitely on the line with this man. She just hoped she wasn't making the biggest mistake of her life.

10

ANGEL

Just as he was about to sit down on the bed beside her, his phone started ringing and he heard the front door open, the house filling with several voices. Jumping up, he pulled his pistol from the back of his pants and looked down at his terrified Little girl. Something was happening and she knew it.

He grabbed his phone and looked at the screen. It was Colt.

"Yeah?" he answered.

"Ash, Beau, and I are downstairs. Someone came creeping in the neighborhood and stopped behind her car. By the time I saw it on the cameras, they were gone, but I checked out her car with a bug detector and it's bugged. He knows she's here. We need to move her immediately."

"Fuck! We'll be down in just a second. Get a car ready, we're going to the gym," Angel told him.

Hanging up the phone, he turned to Nora. "Baby, I need you to change out of your pajamas and into some clothes as quickly as you can. We need to go, baby. We're pretty sure

Trevor knows you're here. I'll tell you everything in the car but please trust me."

She nodded, tears in her eyes as he moved to the dresser and quickly found a pair of leggings and a soft T-shirt for her to wear, tossing them her way.

"I need a bra," she said, looking around the room.

He spotted her bra and handed it to her. "I'm not leaving you alone in here, but I'll stand by the door and look out at the hallway while you get dressed."

She didn't argue and as he stood in the doorway, he could hear her moving around to get dressed. He hated that he wasn't the one doing it for her, especially as bad as she'd been shaking when she'd taken her bra from him.

"Okay," she murmured.

He turned around and grabbed the pair of white Converse tennis shoes he'd bought her, then put them on her feet and laced them. Without asking, he picked her up and carried her out of the room.

As soon as they got to the bottom of the stairs, his brothers surrounded them, all three of them with guns in their hands.

"Wolf is outside waiting for us in his truck," Beau told him.

Nodding, they all left the house, the men looking in every direction for any sign of danger while Nora clung to him tightly, her face buried in his neck.

Lucy was strapped into the back seat of the truck looking worried as Angel climbed in next to her with Nora and Beau got into the front seat.

"We're bringing Kylie and Ava. Everyone else is on their way already. We'll be right behind you," Ash told them.

Wolf started driving, the cab of the truck eerily quiet for the first several minutes.

"I'm sorry," Nora whispered.

She was on his lap and even though he probably should have strapped her in, he didn't want to let her go. She was shaking uncontrollably.

Lowering his face to her ear, he tightened his hold on her. "Don't ever be sorry for something that isn't your fault. You're safe with us, baby girl. I'm going to protect you."

Pulling his phone from his pocket, he looked for a name and hit the call button.

"Yeah?"

"Declan, this is Angel. One of our women is being threatened and we need some extra protection on all of them for a while. Can you spare some men?"

"Killian, round up a dozen of our men and have them ready," Declan called out.

Angel could hear Killian immediately calling out orders in the background.

"Thank you. We have a situation and we don't know how severe it is yet," Angel told him.

"Where do you need them?" Declan asked.

"Send them to the gym."

He carried Nora into the gym. She'd tried to wiggle free, but he told her no and she stopped. He wasn't letting her out of his reach. Not anytime soon. Not until they found this fucker.

"What is this?" she asked quietly.

"It's Beau's gym. We have some secure rooms in the back. We use parts of the gym for prepping for jobs and having meetings. It's safe here," he told her as they followed Beau down one of the long halls with Wolf behind them, carrying Lucy on his hip.

Beau used his fingerprint and then a retina scanner to

unlock the room and when they stepped inside, already several of his brothers, Pop, and their Littles were there.

The relief on Ellie's face when she saw Nora pulled at his heart. Ellie leaped off Hawk's lap and ran over to them, hugging Nora tightly as soon as he set her on her feet.

"You're okay!" Ellie said.

Nora nodded, looking up into Angel's eyes with a lost but trusting gaze that made his heart squeeze in his chest. She hadn't met the entire family yet, and he'd hoped to ease her into it, but that option was out the window. He gave her lower back a small squeeze of support then leaned over and kissed the top of her head.

Colt, Ash, Kylie, and Ava showed up last, and when they closed the door and sat down, a hush fell over the room as everyone looked to Colt.

"I'm sorry. I have nothing. The only thing I have is the make and model of the car. The person had on a hat and hoodie and the plates were removed," Colt told them.

Angel scrubbed his hand over his face. "This fucking bastard has some balls to come out in broad daylight."

The men all nodded while the women sat quietly, most of them clinging to their Daddies in one way or another. It wasn't the first time a situation had occurred where they'd all had to bring their Littles' into this room, but the women knew when it happened that shit was serious.

"We need to lock down. Declan is sending men to help protect the girls. We need to get Nora to a different location and her car needs to get moved into a totally different direction to try to throw him off," Angel told everyone.

Knox cleared his throat. "Nora, I'm Knox. This is my wife, Addie. Sorry we haven't met before now."

Nora tightened her hand around Angel's and looked up at him.

"It's okay, baby girl. You don't have to talk," he said so quietly only she could hear him.

The last thing he'd ever want to do is embarrass her or have her feeling bad for being shy.

Ash smiled at Nora. "I'm Ash. This is Kylie."

Maddox, who was one of the less threatening looking of all his brothers, walked over to Nora and squatted down to her level, smiling warmly. "I'm Maddox. My Little girl over there is Brynn. She's feeling a bit non-verbal today, but I know she's looking forward to meeting you."

Nora eyed Maddox before glancing behind him to where Brynn was sitting with a small blanket in her hands and a pacifier in her mouth. Brynn gave a small wave causing Nora to return a wave.

Angel smiled at his brother, thankful for him trying to make Nora feel comfortable with the fact that she was almost non-verbal around them as well.

One by one, each of the men, including Pop, introduced themselves to her. She smiled at each of them and nodded her understanding. Between Angel, Hawk, and Ellie, the rest of the family knew she wouldn't likely speak to them until she knew them a little bit better. Angel was so damn thankful for the family he had because they'd all accepted it without issue and would still treat her as part of the family no matter what.

Colt opened his laptop and walked over to where Angel had sat down with Nora beside him. Colt pulled up the camera footage and showed it to him and Nora. "Nora, can you tell if this is Trevor?"

She stared at it for several seconds before she nodded. "It's him."

Taking the laptop away, Colt sat down. "Nora, I tried to find information on Trevor. I looked him up by first and last name and searched the police database for his name but came up empty. I think he may have given you a false name."

Her eyebrows furrowed, and she shook her head, looking up at Angel. "I saw his ID. It said his name on it."

Unfortunately, Angel and Colt knew that meant nothing. Fake IDs were easy to get, and unless you knew what to look for, they looked totally real.

"Do you know for sure he was a cop?" Colt asked.

She nodded, moving closer to Angel as if she was searching for his protection. "He drove a police car when we lived here. I saw his badge."

Colt smiled and nodded. "Do you remember any of the numbers on his badge?"

Angel was glad Colt was talking to her. He was one of the less intimidating-looking brothers, though his looks were deceiving. He was just as deadly and tough as the rest of them, but he was easy to talk to. Not quite as gruff as some of them.

"I don't remember. I never looked at it closely. I'm so sorry," she said quietly, looking down at her trembling hands.

Reaching out, Colt gently put his hand on both of hers. "It's okay, sweetheart. This is his fault, not yours. We'll find him, one way or another. Our biggest concern is keeping you safe in the meantime."

Angel watched as Nora raised her gaze to Colt with the saddest looking expression and nodded.

Hawk spoke up next. "Nora, when you watched that video, how did you know it was him?"

Nora looked up at Angel. Leaning down, he put his mouth near her ear. "Whisper to Daddy how you knew it was him."

Her eyes widened and he realized he'd called himself

Daddy, but he wasn't about to take it back. He was in full Daddy mode right now, whether she was officially his or not. He lowered his ear to her mouth and waited.

"He has a slight limp on his right side from getting shot on the job," she whispered into his ear.

Fuck, yes.

"Do you know when he got shot? Around what year? Was it when he was a cop here in Seattle?" Angel whispered back.

She nodded. "I think it happened like five years ago when he first started working as a cop."

Grinning at her, he gently cupped her face and pressed a gentle kiss on her forehead, not giving a fuck that his entire family was watching. When he pulled away, he stared into her eyes. "I'm so proud of you, baby girl. This information is really helpful."

Her eyes were wide and her cheeks flushed.

After relaying what she'd told him to the rest of the family, Colt started typing feverishly on his laptop. "I'll search through the injury database. If he's telling the truth and he was truly shot on the job, his information would be in there. We might need her to look at photos of officers depending on how many we find."

Angel nodded. "In the meantime, I'm moving her into my house. This guy has no way of knowing we're all related so he would have no idea she's staying only a few houses away."

Nora's head snapped back as she stared up at him in surprise. He looked down at her and gave her a stern look. "Baby girl, I will give you a choice in almost everything in this world except when it comes to your health and safety. You're coming to stay with me where you'll be safer."

What he didn't add was that he'd also be able to Daddy her while she was there and give her a peek into what it would be like to be his. She would find out soon enough. He just hoped he could be everything she wanted and needed because his sweet Little girl deserved the world. She'd been through hell, and he wanted to become her heaven. Her guardian Angel.

11

NORA

Everything was happening so fast it felt like a blur. Angel reached out and cupped her chin gently. "I will take care of everything, Little girl. Just trust me and let me take care of you and keep you safe, okay? I promise I will keep you safe."

Without thinking, she nodded. Angel didn't seem like the kind of man to make promises he wouldn't keep. "Okay. I trust you."

He nodded and turned to the rest of the women in the room. "As of right now, all of you girls are on lockdown. This means no going anywhere, not even stepping out of the house, without one of us or a bodyguard with you. Are we clear on this?"

One by one, each of the women nodded. It was obvious this wasn't the first time they'd experienced something like this, and it was also obvious they knew how serious the situation was.

Colt looked up from his laptop. "Declan, Killian, and their men are here."

Beau nodded and walked out of the room, returning a

moment later with over a dozen men who looked just as terrifying as Angel and his brothers. These men were all dressed in well fitted, expensive looking black suits, though.

She noticed a tall man standing slightly in front of the other men. Even though his black suit fit him like a glove, she could tell he was muscular. The most remarkable thing about him, though, were his eyes. They were the most vibrant green she'd ever seen with a dark ring around the edge of the iris. She shivered. He was handsome, but there was a kind of dangerous magnetism about him, and she found him both attractive and terrifying at the same time.

"What are we dealing with?" the man asked.

Angel nodded toward her. "Declan, this is Nora."

The man she now knew as Declan looked at her and his expression instantly darkened. "Hello, sweet girl," he said before turning toward Angel. "And I see we're going to kill the motherfucker who hurt this Little girl?"

"Yep," Angel answered.

Declan nodded. "Got it."

Another man, nearly the same height as Declan stepped forward, his expression completely emotionless. But when she looked into his eyes, she could see a mix of rage and compassion. He nodded toward her. "I'm Killian. I'm so sorry someone hurt you," he told her before turning toward Angel. "You have our men at your disposal. You can always bring the girls to one of our safe houses if you need to. If you need any resources, just ask. Do you know who this person is?"

Colt shook his head. "He gave her a fake name. We have nothing to go on except that he is or was at one point a cop who got shot here in Washington. He bugged her car and showed up at Hawk's house today where she's staying. He got out just briefly and walked around her car and checked out the house, just seeming to be observing the place. We're moving her to Angel's place but at this point, we're trying to find him with the information we have. We need her car relocated somewhere that if he follows it again, he could be easily trapped and held."

Declan looked at one of the other suited men who was standing beside him. "Get someone to go get her car from Hawk's and move it to one of the safe houses. Have someone move it each day. We'll send this bastard on a wild-goose chase."

The man nodded and pulled his cell phone from inside his suit jacket, stepping off to the side to make a call.

She didn't know what to think about all these people jumping in to help her. In her entire life, the only person who had ever been there for her was Ellie, and now a bunch of men she didn't even know were doing whatever they could to keep her safe. It was a strange feeling.

Angel stood and walked over to Declan, shaking his hand. "I owe you."

Declan smiled and shook his head. "No, you don't. We help each other out when needed. Besides, you know I fucking hate abusers and people who hurt women. I just hope I get to watch as you gut his body."

Angel smiled, though it wasn't the kind of smile that gave her the warm fuzzies. No, it was a smile that probably made people run in the other direction. "I'm sure that can be arranged."

A shiver ran through her. Whoever Declan was, he was dangerous. Very, very dangerous.

Walking back to her, Angel grabbed hold of her hand and pulled her up to stand. "Let's go home, baby girl."

Warmth spread through her entire body. Home. It was a word that most people didn't give a second thought about, but was a place she'd always dreaded going. Why wasn't she dreading it now? She knew the answer to that; the answer was she was going there with Angel. How had this man she barely knew become her safe haven?

———

THEY WERE ESCORTED home by two of the suited men in a black SUV. Angel hadn't wanted them to return in the same truck they'd left in just in case there was anyone hanging around their neighborhood that shouldn't have been. The drive back to the house was quiet, with only the occasional sound from a passing vehicle or the two men in the front of the SUV talking quietly with what she was pretty sure were Irish accents. When they finally arrived at Angel's house, which was just as large and beautiful as Hawk's, the men made sure that everything was secure before allowing them to enter the house. Nora let out a sigh of relief as she heard the door lock behind them.

Angel turned to her in the foyer and looked down at her with a concerned expression. "Are you okay, baby girl?"

No. She wasn't. Not even close to being okay. Trevor had put a bug on her car and if she hadn't had Angel and his brothers keeping such a close eye on her and the neighborhood, who knows what would have happened. What if she hadn't gone to Ellie's and gone somewhere else by herself? Trevor probably would have found her and killed her.

Suddenly, it was all too much to take. She started sobbing, her legs giving out from under her as the weight of everything became too heavy to process. Before she could fall to the floor, she was in Angel's arms being carried through the house. She was crying too hard to see where they were going but it didn't matter. Angel would take care of her.

He sat down with her on his lap, his arms wrapped

around her as she cried. He said nothing, just held and rocked her gently as if he were soothing a baby. Eventually, the tears subsided, and she was able to look up at him.

He smiled down at her, his eyes full of compassion and understanding. "It's okay," he said softly. "I know it's been hard. I know you're feeling overwhelmed and lost. But I'm here, and I won't let anything bad happen to you."

She smiled weakly in return, grateful for his understanding and reassurance. She leaned against him, feeling the warmth of his embrace and the security it provided her. How was she ever going to be able to walk away from this man once it was all over? Surely he wouldn't want her forever. He barely knew her. Once he realized what a mess she was, he would decide she was too much of a burden and move on.

She sighed heavily, feeling the tears threaten to sting her eyes again. He held her tighter against him and kissed the top of her head. "It's going to be alright, baby girl," he murmured soothingly in her ear.

She wanted so desperately to believe him, but she was too scared.

He pulled back slightly, hooking his finger under her chin so she was looking into his eyes. "I know you don't believe me right now, but I'm telling you the truth. You can get through this. We will get through this together, no matter what happens. And I'm going to show you what having a real, loving Daddy is like. You're going to be my girl, Nora. Maybe not today, but I will do whatever it takes to show you I'll never hurt you."

She nodded and sniffed, feeling completely drained and too tired to move, but surely he didn't want her sitting on his lap all day. When she tried to wiggle free, he tightened his arms around her and shook his head. "If you need to go somewhere, tell me where and I'll take you."

"I don't need to go anywhere. I just don't want to be a bother to you. You've been so nice to me and I'm just such a mess, Angel. I have things inside me that I don't know if I'll ever get over. I'll never be normal."

He stared at her for a long moment before his lips spread into a smile and he chuckled, shaking his head. "Baby girl, what does normal even mean anyway? Do you think I'm normal? None of us are normal and all of us have trauma. I still fight my own demons every single day. And I'm prepared to help you fight yours because I care about you, Little girl. I am drawn to you like a magnet and I know I probably sound crazy for saying this, but I know deep down in my soul that you are the one for me. I don't care if there's shit you never get over or heal from. I will learn how to navigate around those things and help you in any way that I can. I don't want fucking normal. That sounds boring. I want you, Little girl."

What. The. Fuck. What was she supposed to say to that? With every declaration he made, it was harder and harder not to have feelings for him. Yeah, as if she didn't already have feelings for him.

"That's...that's a lot," she managed to choke out after a few moments of silence. "I don't know what to say."

His thumb stroked her jawline. "Say you'll at least keep an open mind and let me take care of you? Let me Daddy you a bit? The real kind of Daddying. No sex. Just care."

Could she let him do that? Being taken care of, the way she'd always fantasized about, sounded heavenly. Ellie had said she could trust him and that all the men were amazing caretakers and Daddies. She couldn't imagine Angel being any different.

Slowly, she nodded her head. "Okay. But I might get scared. Or panic. Or do something wrong."

His dark eyes softened. "Oh, baby girl. I'm going to

teach you that it's okay to do things wrong. Or to panic. Or be scared. And each time any of those things happen, we will work through it together. You're not alone anymore, Nora. Even if you decide you don't want me, you will always be a part of this family now. You will always have a place here."

Letting out a long, deep breath, she nodded and lowered her head to his chest, letting the warmth of him soothe her as he ran his hand up and down her back until she couldn't keep her eyes open any longer.

12

ANGEL

Holding her in his arms was quickly becoming his favorite thing in the world. When he held her, it seemed to make all the unwanted thoughts and noise inside his head go quiet.

It had been a long, exhausting day and now the entire family was on lockdown until they found this crazy fuck. Keeping their women safe was always their first priority. As his brothers had started meeting their Littles, the men had all talked about stopping what they did in the shadows. They didn't want to take any chances on getting killed, arrested, or worse, one of their girls getting hurt. When they'd talked to the women, though, the men had been told not to quit because there were people out there who really needed them. And that was true. There were always people out there who needed saving, but the most important thing in their lives now was their women. And Nora had already became the most important thing in Angel's life.

He wished he knew all she'd been through and in time, he hoped she would share all of that with him, but it really didn't matter because he'd meant what he had said. He would work through everything with her. She wasn't alone anymore. He'd take care of her and protect her. Always.

———————

It was past dinnertime when she finally opened her eyes and looked up at him. He hadn't moved from the couch, and he would have sat there all night with her if it meant she was getting some peaceful sleep. One thing he planned to start doing was getting her on a schedule for naps and bedtime so she would get plenty of rest. He also hoped being on a schedule would make her feel more secure.

"Hey, sleepyhead. How's my girl?"

A small smile spread on her lips as she brought her fists up to her eyes, rubbing the sleep away. "How long did I sleep?"

He shrugged. "A couple of hours. I bet you're a hungry Little girl, huh?"

Letting out a contented sigh, she nodded. "Kinda."

Angel chuckled and got up, setting her on her feet. "Come on. Why don't you go potty and I'll start dinner. How do you feel about pancakes?"

Nora giggled softly. "Yummy."

"I thought so, too. Go potty."

Nodding, she scampered off to the bathroom. She emerged a few minutes later looking much more awake and content.

He smiled at her as he mixed up pancake batter and when she walked into the kitchen, he stopped and handed her a sippy cup of juice he'd poured for her. "You haven't had much to drink today. I want you to drink as much of that as you can."

"Thank you," she said with a smile before taking a sip.

He watched her as he finished making the pancakes

and when it was time to eat, they both sat down at the table together. "Oh wow! These are really yummy!" Nora moaned after taking a bite.

His cock instantly hardened at the sound and he had to give himself a silent pep-talk to calm the fuck down before she saw his hard-on through his jeans. The last thing he wanted to do was scare her away.

"After dinner, how about a bath and a movie before bed?"

Her green eyes lit up as she nodded. "Will you watch a movie with me?"

Leaning forward so his face was closer to hers, he met her gaze. "Of course I will, Little one. I'd give you a bath if I thought you'd be comfortable with it. You'll come to learn that I love being a Daddy and I'll want to spend as much time with you as I can both for fun and to take care of you."

Her cheeks turned pink and she lowered her gaze from his, poking her fork at her food. Slowly, he reached over with his own fork and cut a piece of the pancake before holding it up to her mouth. She stared at it for a long moment before she accepted the bite. It felt so intimate feeding her and it pleased him that she was letting him. It was something so small, but she was giving him a tiny bit of her trust at a time. He continued to feed her one bite after another until the plate was cleared and she had a satisfied smile on her face.

He smiled back and reached for her hand, giving it a gentle squeeze. "Thank you for trusting me enough to let me feed you." She gave him a small nod and leaned into his touch. He knew they still had a long way to go in their relationship, but this moment would stay with him forever. This small gesture of trust meant more than any words could ever express.

Just as he finished clearing their dishes, his phone

chimed with a text letting him know one of Declan's men was outside with Nora's belongings. They had gone through every single thing she had to make sure there were no other bugs planted.

Holding the bags up, he nodded toward the stairs. "Let's go up and get comfy and then we can relax."

She nodded and followed him up the stairs. He really wanted to go directly into his own room and put her stuff down there, but that would be moving too fast, so he went into the guest bedroom closest to his. Eventually, he would turn it into a playroom for her, but for now, it was set up as a regular room.

He set the bags down on the bed and turned around to find her standing shyly off to the side with her arms wrapped around her middle. He took slow steps toward her until he stopped just a few inches away. She looked up at him with an uncertain expression.

"There's a big tub in the attached bathroom and there's bubble bath under the sink. I'll let you bathe yourself this time but I want you to take your phone in with you and leave the bathroom door ajar so you can call out if you need me. I'll be in my bedroom so you can have privacy. Do you need anything else?"

Letting out a slow breath, she did something that surprised the hell out of him. She stepped forward and wrapped her arms around his waist, her face resting against his chest. He froze at first, surprised by her, then wrapped his arms around her, hugging her tightly.

"Thank you, Angel. I've never felt so safe."

A lump formed in his throat as he lowered his face and kissed the top of her head. "I'm glad you feel safe with me, baby," he said as smoothly as he could muster.

When she released him and stepped back, she was smiling and he felt as though he was on top of the world.

He hadn't done a lot of things right in his life, but he would get this right. Even if it took forever. She deserved everything and so much more and the Daddy side of him knew with absolute certainty that she was his Little girl.

"Go take a bath and relax, baby girl. Call out if you need me."

Nodding, she turned around and went into the ensuite bathroom, leaving him standing in the middle of the room with a wide smile on his face.

Leaving the guest room, Angel walked into his bedroom and ran a hand over his face. His cock was so painfully hard it wasn't even funny. No one, not one single woman that he'd ever dated or played with, had turned him on the way Nora did. One look from her and that's all it took for his cock to wake up and join the party. It really needed to chill out because sex wasn't even close to being on the table with her. He had to move slowly. Give her time to trust him and understand that what he wanted with her wasn't just a sexual game. Once she understood that and she was ready, he'd make her scream over and over again.

After changing into a pair of sweats and a soft T-shirt, he sat in one of the overstuffed chairs near the fireplace in his bedroom and called Colt.

"Hey."

"Please tell me you found something?"

Colt grunted. "Sorry, bro. Still weeding through injury reports. I was able to find out the apartment they were renting was leased to a Trevor Thomas. Her name wasn't on the lease. Declan has some men who live in that area so he sent them to check out the apartment for us, but they didn't find anything. All the mail they found was for Trevor Thomas. This guy had a whole fucking identity under that name except for at work apparently. It's crazy. I don't even know where to go from here, but I'll keep searching."

Angel sighed. He wasn't sure what else could be done. "Thanks, bro. I appreciate you dropping everything for this."

Colt scoffed. "She's family. You know we protect our family at all costs. How's she doing, by the way?"

Looking toward his open bedroom door, he sighed. "She's as good as can be. I hate that she's going through this and I want to take all of her pain away, but I can't so I feel kind of helpless."

"You might not be able to take her pain away, Angel, but you can be there for her, and you know just as well as I do that having someone that's there for you helps more than most people realize. She'll learn that you're a safe person. Maybe tomorrow or the next day I'll bring Ava over for a bit so they can get to know each other. It sounds like Ellie has been her only friend in her life so I'm betting she could use a few more."

Angel felt a surge of appreciation for Colt. "I love you, brother."

"I love you, too. I'll call you as soon as I find out anything."

Hanging up the phone, he heard a soft knock and when he looked up, he saw Nora standing in the doorway in a matching set of pajamas he'd bought her. Her long brown hair was wet, and she'd braided it into two braids at the base of her neck.

"Hey, pretty girl. How was your bath?" he asked, motioning for her to come in.

She looked around shyly as she took a step into the bedroom. "It was good. I could have fallen asleep in there it was so relaxing."

Furrowing his eyebrows, he crooked his finger for her to come to him. She moved slowly but when she was finally close enough for him to reach out and touch her, he pulled her onto his lap. "No falling asleep in the tub, Little girl. This is why Daddies usually give their Little girls a bath."

Her green eyes met his and they stared at each other in silence for a long moment before he slowly lowered his face and brushed his lips against hers. She let out a quiet gasp but didn't pull away. Not wanting to push her too far, he pulled back and stroked his thumb over her plump lips. "You're absolutely breathtaking, Nora. I'm trying so hard to move slow but I'm struggling. I want to Daddy you so bad. You'll need to let me know if I'm coming on too strongly, okay?"

Her tongue darted out to wet her lips as she stared up at him. "You're not. I... I kind of like it. You make me feel wanted," she whispered.

Wrapping his hand around the back of her neck, he squeezed the sides gently. "That's because you *are* wanted, baby."

13

NORA

He wanted her. She wanted him, too. She wanted everything he told her he wanted to give her, but she was scared. What was the worst that could happen? She'd already been through hell with her father and then with Trevor. How much worse could it possibly get? It couldn't, so why not take a chance?

Looking down at his muscular arm, she traced the lines of his dark tattoos with her finger while she tried to gather her thoughts. "Everything you say about wanting to be my Daddy, I want those things, too. I want to have what Ellie has with Hawk. I see how much he loves and adores her, and I see how safe and happy she feels. I want those feelings, too. But what if... what if I can't give you everything you need? What if I can't ever talk to your family because I'm too shy or what if I'm not enough for you?"

Angel shifted her so she was cradled in his arms like a baby. It was a strange feeling having him move her around as if she weighed nothing. She was short but she wasn't light, not that he seemed to mind. Even she saw the way he looked at her sometimes.

"First of all, Little girl, if you can't ever talk to my family, they will still love and accept you for you. They'll text you if they have to so they can communicate. I'm not sure if you've noticed, but the people in my family are all different. The Littles in our family are all different. We all accept and love one another no matter what. Secondly, you're already enough for me just as you are. You're sweet and smart and strong. Baby, you're so damn strong."

Reaching up, she ran her fingers over the short scruff of his beard. It was soothing and she didn't want to pull her hand away. He didn't seem to mind, though, because he leaned into her hand then moved his face so he could press a kiss into the palm of her hand, his dark eyes trained on hers.

"You don't have to decide anything right now, Nora. I'm not going anywhere, baby. And even if I'm not officially your Daddy, I won't be able to help Daddying you because I know you're my Little girl. But if I'm ever Daddying you too much or you want me to back off, you just tell me and I will always respect your boundaries. Okay?"

Wow. She was starting to wonder if he'd come from an alternate universe because this man was something else. "Okay," she whispered.

He smiled down at her and stood with her in his arms as he carried her over to the bed and set her down. "It's up to you but how about watching a movie in my bed? We can get comfy and relax. I promise not to touch you."

She looked up at him and nodded. She wanted him to touch her, though. She was already missing the heat of his chest against her.

He pulled the blankets back and motioned for her to get comfortable then crawled in next to her. He scooted close enough for them both to be comfortable while still keeping a safe distance between them. He grabbed the remote from his nearby nightstand and started a movie.

They snuggled into the blankets, leaning back against the pillows as they watched the movie. She couldn't help but feel relaxed next to him, her body gradually melting into his side with each passing minute. His warmth and the scent of his cologne made her feel safe and secure. About halfway through the movie, she shifted and rested her head on his chest, smiling when he lifted his arm and wrapped it around her.

When the movie ended, he turned off the TV as they both just lay there in silence. He tightened his arm around her, pulling her into him. She felt herself relax even more as she let go of all her worries and smoothed her hand over his hard chest. The man was ripped. She wondered if he was completely covered in tattoos under his T-shirt as well. One thing was obvious, Angel and his brothers weren't afraid of needles.

"What do you call a sad berry?" Angel asked, breaking their silence.

A smile crept over her face and she let out a laugh. She had no idea where he came up with these jokes, but she could swear with each one she fell for him a little more. "I don't know. What do you call it?"

"A blueberry," he said, tickling her side.

She burst out laughing from both the joke and the tickling and when she threw her head back and looked up at him, he was grinning down at her. Both of them froze as they stared at each other, their expressions quickly changing from laughing to serious and suddenly, it felt like the air between them was sizzling.

Angel cupped her face, stroking her uninjured cheek with his thumb as he lowered his mouth to hers and pressed a soft kiss to her lips. Sliding her hand up his chest, she snaked it around the back of his neck and kissed him back. She liked that he was definitely leading the kiss but not forcing it and the longer it went on, the deeper it became until she parted her lips for him and he started exploring her mouth. A small moan escaped her as he nipped at her bottom lip before pulling back and meeting her gaze again.

Holy wowza. That kiss was... everything. More than anything she could have ever fantasized about and definitely better than anything she'd ever experienced.

"I need to get you to bed, Little girl."

Her heart fell into her stomach. Did he not like it? Why did he want to get rid of her so suddenly? She tried to pull away but he held her firmly, his eyebrows pulling together.

"I want you to sleep in here with me. I'll sleep on the floor if you want me to, but I can't stand the thought of being away from you."

Oh. Well. Huh. Nevermind those negative thoughts. He wanted to sleep in the same room as her? She couldn't help but blush at the thought and she nodded timidly.

She was rewarded with a breathtaking smile that made her squeeze her thighs together. How she was going to spend the night in the same room as him and actually sleep, she had no idea.

Angel got up out of bed and held out his hand. "Come on. Why don't you go potty and brush your teeth while I make a bed on the floor."

Reaching out, she put her hand in his and let him help her up but as she stood in front of him, she stared up at him, unmoving. "Maybe... um... you could sleep in the bed, too? I won't take up much room."

His eyes burned into her and he lifted his hand to gently hold her chin. "Baby girl, you can take up as much of the bed as you want and it won't bother me a bit. I'd love to sleep in bed with you."

She couldn't hide the smile that automatically spread across her face. Her cheeks were warm at the thought of sharing a bed with Angel but to be honest, her entire body was warm and had been ever since she'd met him.

Leaning forward, Angel kissed her forehead. "Go potty, baby. I'll go grab your hippo from the other room. Anything else you need?"

The consideration of this man. She just couldn't believe he was real. She shook her head. "No. Thank you."

He winked at her and nudged her toward his bathroom where she closed the door and quickly used the toilet. A few seconds later there was a light knock on the door, and when she opened it, Angel was standing there looking like sex on a stick as he leaned against the doorframe.

"Here's your toothbrush. There's toothpaste in the middle drawer. Use anything else you need in there, and if there's anything else you need, I'll get it for you tomorrow."

She took her toothbrush from him and stepped back, turning toward the vanity. He didn't move, and when she was done brushing her teeth, he was still standing there watching her with an intrigued expression on his face.

"What?" she asked, slightly embarrassed.

He shrugged and stepped away from the doorframe, taking her hand in his as he led her out of the bathroom.

"I like being close to you," he admitted.

When they approached the bed, she saw both the hippo he'd given her and the small stuffed bear the doctor had given her. Right next to them was a lavender colored pacifier. She eyed it then looked up at him nervously. He shrugged, almost looking a little unsure. "I wasn't sure if you'd like to use one so I ordered some for you. Have you used a pacifier before?"

She nodded slowly, looking back down at it. Pacifiers were one of her favorite Little things to use for soothing her anxiety. When she raised her gaze again to meet Angel's, he was smiling softly.

"Use it, baby girl. I want you to be able to be as Little as you want to be. You'll learn that I'm the type of Daddy who likes to have full control so if you let me, I'll be picking out your clothes each day, dressing you, bathing you, feeding you, diapering you at times, and more. But I'll only take as much control as you'll allow me. Just don't be afraid to be Little with me because I love seeing it. Okay?"

"'Kay."

He winked at her and motioned to the bed. "Climb in, baby girl."

She did and when she was settled under the covers, he handed her the stuffed hippo and pulled the covers up higher. When he leaned over and kissed her forehead, she sighed contentedly.

Angel walked around to the other side of the bed, pulled off his shirt, and got under the covers, keeping his distance from her. After he turned off the bedside lamp much too quickly, he lay on his back with one arm up over his head and the other at his side. He'd left the light on in the bathroom and left the door open a crack so she was able to see his profile, and even in the dim lighting he was so handsome. Despite his tattoos, scars, and intimidating appearance, he was a beautiful man. She really had no idea why he was interested in her, but she was too sleepy to question it.

"Sweet dreams, baby girl."

"Night, Angel," she whispered before she picked up the pacifier and slid it between her lips.

SOMETHING WAS TICKLING her nose and it was really disrupting the peaceful sleep she'd been getting. Swiping at her face, she let out a sound of distress as whatever it was continued to tickle.

The pillow she was sleeping on started shaking and she realized her head wasn't on a pillow.

"Do I need to shave my chest so it doesn't tickle your face, baby girl?"

Her eyes sprang open, and she lifted her head to find Angel looking down at her with a grin across his face. Her mouth dropped open, causing the pacifier that was still in her mouth to fall out onto his chest.

"Morning, baby girl."

Holy hell. His voice was even deeper than normal from sleep, making her nipples instantly bud under her pajamas. When had she become such a hornball?

"Morning," she murmured, grabbing the pacifier and setting it off to the side.

He reached out and started stroking her head. "You seemed to sleep well."

Yeah, she had. It had been the first really good night's rest she'd had in a long time. When had she moved over to his side and snuggled up against him? He was still on his side of the bed, so it was obvious she had sought him out.

Lowering her head to his chest again, she sighed softly. "I slept really good."

Angel continued to stroke her head for several minutes as they lay in silence.

"Guess you'll have to start sleeping with Daddy every night then, huh?" he finally asked.

Without even thinking, she nodded her head. "Yeah."

14

ANGEL

She wasn't the only one who'd slept well. He'd slept better than he'd slept in years. No nightmares plagued him and he hadn't woken up several times through the night like he normally did. In fact, the only time he'd woken was when she'd moved over and wrapped herself around him. He'd tensed up at first, but after a few seconds the warmth of her body and her steady breathing had soothed him back to sleep.

If it were up to him, he would keep her in bed with him all day and snuggle, but he knew both of them needed to get work done. He had some fights he needed to watch and analyze and he knew she was in the middle of editing a romance novel and was worried about getting behind because of everything that had been going on.

He just wasn't ready to end the moment, though. Even though they weren't really talking, it still felt as though they were so incredibly close and the fact that she was the one willingly resting her head on top of him wasn't something he was going to interrupt.

"Baby girl," he murmured.

"Hmm?"

"Tell me, when you think about the perfect Daddy, what is he like?"

She traced the lines of one of his tattoos on his bicep for several seconds before she answered him.

"He loves and accepts me unconditionally. He's patient and kind. He's protective and caring. He truly loves being a Daddy and he doesn't make me feel bad for being a needy Little. He reads me stories and tells me silly jokes."

A smile pulled at his lips at the last part. Had she said that just because of him? It didn't matter either way because he would tell her silly jokes for the rest of their lives just to see the twinkle in her eye and her smile.

"What is your perfect Little like?" she asked quietly.

Tightening his arm around her, he stroked her head. "She's sweet and strong. Loving. She loves me despite my own demons. She lets me take care of her and Daddy her. She knows I'm not perfect but still loves me and looks up to me anyway. She trusts me. She knows I'd do anything for her to take care of her and protect her. She has brown hair, beautiful round hips, the greenest eyes I've ever seen, and when she smiles, she has the cutest little dimples. She's scared and damaged, but she's perfect for me because so am I."

Nora's finger froze and she lifted her head, peering up at him from under her lashes. "You don't seem very damaged. Not like me."

He stared down at her for a long moment before deciding whether or not he should explain his past to her. It might make her understand him better and he knew it also might make her feel more comfortable with sharing her past with him.

Letting out a sigh, he gave her a sad smile. "When I was a kid, I had to watch my mom be beaten and raped repeatedly by my dad and his friends. I was young, maybe only four or five the first time I remember seeing it happen. She'd dated my dad in high school and got pregnant when she was seventeen. My father was a gangster. He sold hard drugs and eventually the gang he was part of started selling women.

"My mom started doing drugs with him and I remember they used to fight like crazy. My dad would hurt my mom. He would beat her and then rape her when she was barely conscious. I was so small, I couldn't do anything. As I got a little older, I started trying to protect my mom, but my father would beat me until I was unconscious.

"He started bringing his friends over to have sex with her and she was so high on the drugs he was shooting into her that she didn't even know what was going on. Our home was filthy and we rarely had food in the house. I was eight the first time my father took me with him to do drug deals. He had me delivering heroine and cocaine to people and I was so young, I knew I had to do it or risk being beaten or killed at the hands of my own father.

"When I was ten, I saw my father and five of his friends rape an underage girl and kill her right afterward. She wasn't even in high school yet. I knew I had to do something because I knew it wasn't right. I needed money to get away and I needed connections so I started dealing drugs on my own. I wasn't even twelve the first time I had to shoot someone. My father pointed a gun to my head and told me to shoot the guy or he was going to shoot me so I shot the guy.

"When I was thirteen, I came home one night to my father and several of his friends beating my mom bloody because she was too high to have sex with them. My father hit her in the head with a hammer, and she died right in front of them. They did nothing. I was screaming and trying to get to her, but they wouldn't let me help her. Instead, they dragged me out and took me to another woman's house where they gave her drugs and got her so high she was barely awake before they started raping her. My father told me to join in, but I told him I wouldn't. I was still screaming and crying about my mom, so he pulled his gun and shot me. The bullet barely missed my vital organs.

"I don't know how, but somehow, I was able to run out of that house and make it almost a block away before I dropped in the middle of the street. Someone found me and called the police. I spent almost six months in the hospital recovering, and every single day I spent there, I swore I would kill my father one day. I hadn't saved my mother or saved any of the other girls I'd seen him hurt and I loathed myself because of it.

"While I was in the hospital, a social worker came to see me. Her name was Sophia Javier and she sat beside my bed almost every other day and talked to me. For the first month she came, I refused to speak to her but she didn't stop coming. She would show up and sit by my bed and talk to me. Before I got released from the hospital, she gave me a business card with the name of her husband's gym and told me if I ever needed anything that I was to go there and he would help me no matter what it was.

"I went into the foster care system and was sent from one shitty family to another. I was angry and caused a lot of trouble because of my anger. I constantly saw visions of my mom being raped, tortured, and killed right in front of me. I blamed myself because I'd never done anything about it. I didn't save my own mother, and I had a gun so I could have killed my father, but I didn't, and I didn't know why.

"I knew I needed to make him pay for what he'd done but I couldn't find him. The police had told me they hadn't been able to find him after he shot me, so I knew he was still on the loose. When I finally tracked him down, I made a plan to kill him, and when I showed up at the house where he was staying with the other guys who had hurt my mom, he was shocked to see me and how big I'd gotten from working out and getting into fights. He tried to talk to me, make me feel like he was glad to see me, but I didn't want to hear any of it. We started fighting, he swung at me first, but once I started throwing punches, everything went black, and by the time I came to, he was dead in the middle of the front yard. The other guys had already run away.

"I ran. I had blood all over me, and my knuckles were bloodied, and even though I'd killed him, he'd still gotten some hits in so I was in bad shape. I don't know how I made it, but I went to the gym. As soon as I walked in, Leo knew exactly who I was. He rushed me into the back and started cleaning me up then called a doctor he knew from the circuit to come stitch me up. He hid me in the gym for weeks until he was able to confirm my father's death was ruled a gang related incident and the case was closed.

"Once I was in the clear, he told me I had to decide if I wanted to go down the same path as my father. When I said no, he told me that if I could keep my fighting in the walls of the gym and stay out of the gang scene, he and his family wanted to have me come live with them. It was hard at first. Leo, Sophia, Beau, Celeste, Knox, Ash, Wolf; all of them just accepted me and loved me from the get-go, but I wasn't used to that kind of life.

"I stayed angry, and I stayed closed off from them for months, but then Leo started training with me in the gym. He drove me there at five in the morning every single day before it opened and the two of us trained together. We sparred, and during those sparring sessions we talked until one day I broke down and bawled like a fucking baby in his arms. He held me for a long time and talked to me, told me my past wasn't my fault and I had no control over what happened with my mom. He told me I did what I needed to do to get justice for my mom and beating myself up over it for the rest of my life would be its own death sentence. I was still angry after that but not as much, and the longer I lived with Pop and Ma, the less angry I got. I took my anger out in the gym on my brothers and when I was eighteen, I asked Pop if I could join the fighting circuit. I think if it had been any of my other brothers asking, he would have said no but I think he knew I needed it, so he let me. It helped a lot."

Realizing he'd been talking for a long time, he stopped and looked down at Nora who was crying, her tears dripping onto his chest. She looked up at him with the saddest expression and his heart tightened in his chest.

"Angel," she cried.

Lifting her hand to his face, she stroked his cheek and he turned his head to kiss her palm. "I'm okay, baby. It's gotten easier over the years. I've spent time with therapists and a lot of time in the ring working out my feelings. I still have guilt and demons inside me but they aren't quite as bad as they used to be."

She shook her head, letting out a sob. "Fuck. I just... That's horrible. I'm so sorry. Here I am, being a baby over the shit that's happened in my life and you, you've been through actual hell."

Reaching down, he cupped her chin and stared into her eyes. "Don't belittle what you've been through just because it's different. It doesn't make it any less of a hell or less traumatic. I told you because I want you to understand me and why I hate abusers so much. I survived what I went through because I was supposed to survive. If I hadn't gone through it, I never would have met the family I have now and I love them so fucking much. They have loved me since day one and have never judged me or loved me less because I wasn't as easy to deal with. Sometimes I think people go through really bad things in their lives so they can appreciate all the good that comes their way even more."

She sighed and rested her head on his chest again, her tears still falling. His own eyes burned with unshed tears.

"I will never hurt you, Nora. Not physically, mentally, or emotionally. Never, baby girl."

"I know," she whispered.

He let out a deep breath and stroked her head as they lay in silence again.

15

NORA

She rested on his chest for a long time in silence, tears slowly falling from her eyes. She couldn't even fathom the horror that Angel had gone through as a child. It was horrendous and instead of turning into a complete monster, he'd made something of himself and used his skills to help innocent people.

Hearing his story made her heart ache for him. Maybe that was why he'd become a Daddy. He wanted to take care of and protect someone because he felt as though he hadn't been able to protect his mom. Then again, she often wondered if she was Little because she'd missed out on so much of a childhood.

He deserved to know about her past. About the horrible things she'd been through so he would know exactly what he was getting himself into. She had a feeling that was why he'd shared his story with her. So she would know what she was getting herself into with him. But if he'd thought his story would have pushed her away, he couldn't have been more wrong because it made her care for him even more. It also made her trust him a little more. She knew he would die before hurting a woman.

Letting out a long slow breath, she gathered her courage and started talking. "My father was a respected doctor in the town we lived in. He was on the city council and owned his own practice, so we lived in a big house with beautiful shutters and a gardener. Everything in our lives was picture perfect. The kids at school were envious of me because I was from one of the wealthiest families in the town we lived. My mother died during my birth, so I never met her. I was raised by my father.

"What people didn't know was my father was an alcoholic with a terrible temper. He believed children shouldn't be seen *or* heard. I was only three or four the first time he beat me for speaking out of turn. He would hit me with anything that was close by. It didn't matter if I was spoken to first, if I replied, I got beaten. He hated me.

"I stopped speaking when I was five. I wouldn't say a word. My father told people I had a form of autism and my not speaking was part of it. He still found reasons to beat me. If I didn't turn the light off when I left a room, if I spilled milk, if I looked at him the wrong way. As I started going to school, he made sure to only beat me in places my clothes would cover and because I had gone completely mute, he knew I wouldn't tell anyone. I was scared to speak to anyone because I thought no matter who I would talk to I would get hit.

"I had no friends, and everyone started thinking I was weird because I never talked to anyone. I never understood why other kids talked so freely, I thought being beaten was normal. That all kids went through it. My father said that was the only way I'd learn.

"I met Ellie in school and she was the only kid who continued to try to be my friend. Her parents had always told her to find the loneliest kid in school and be friends with them, so she became my friend. I don't think I spoke one word to her for the first year of our friendship, but it didn't stop her from sitting with me at lunch every day. She would tell me all about her day or what she did with her family the night before or whatever was on her mind, and never expected me to talk back.

"The day I turned thirteen, my father started coming into my bedroom at night. I was so afraid, and I knew if I said anything or cried that it would make it worse, so I never did anything. He told me it was his job as a doctor to give me a daily exam. Every night for the next five years he came into my bedroom and touched me while he did stuff to himself. He knew I was so scared out of my mind that I would never say anything. He told me if I ever told anyone he would put me in a cage and never let me out, and the thought of not being able to go to school each day to get away from that house was enough for me to never speak a word of it."

She had to pause to take several deep breaths as tears poured out of her onto his chest. Angel's hand had stilled, and she could hear his heavy breathing, but she couldn't look up at him.

"I never told Ellie what my father was doing to me but she knew something was wrong in my life. She knew my reasons for being so quiet stemmed from more than just being shy or having autism. The night her parents died in the fire was one of the first times she'd ever been to my house. My father had gone out of town for a night to attend a conference, so she showed up and told me she was staying the night with me.

"She walked in while I was changing into my pajamas, saw the bruises on my body and cried, apologizing to me over and over for never realizing that my own father was hurting me. We were seventeen, and I knew when I was eighteen I could be free of him. I didn't know how I was going to do it, but I didn't care, either. I would live on the streets if I had to. Ellie told me she was going to talk to her parents the next day because they would help do whatever it took to get me away from my father.

"She got the call in the middle of the night about her parents dying in a house fire. She was supposed to go into foster care until she turned eighteen but she didn't want to, so we made a plan to run away to Seattle. We were only six months away from turning eighteen, so we just had to hide until then. We left in the middle of the night and never looked back. It was terrifying but also freeing. I was free of the cage I'd been in all my life. I was free of all the abuse and hurt. Ellie looked out for me and never treated me like a burden because I couldn't talk to people like she could. She got us out of a lot of tricky situations and found us jobs we were able to do under the table until we turned eighteen.

"Things were good. She went to school and I learned how to use computers and started getting into editing. I didn't have to talk to people to do that job so it worked well for me. I felt on top of the world and slowly started feeling like I was becoming my own person. Then I met Trevor and shared my history with him. It was easy to share because we spoke online for the first several months. He must have realized that I was an easy target. I was so stupid."

Letting out a sob, she brought a hand to her face and tried to wipe the falling tears, but they just kept coming.

Angel shifted, pulling himself to sit up with his back resting against the headboard. He moved her so she was cradled in his arms, looking up at him. His dark eyes stared down at her with so much emotion.

"First of all, Little girl, you are not stupid. I never want to hear you call yourself a name like that again. You are brave and fucking strong as hell. Fuck. I can't believe you went through that. You went through hell, baby. Fuck. Goddammit. I wish I could have protected you."

He was so visibly upset that she reached up to touch his beard, causing him to look down at her, tears in his eyes. Shaking his head, his body trembled as he held her and together, they both cried silently as they clung to each other.

They'd both been through hell. Absolute hell.

After Angel swiped away his tears, his eyes darkened and his eyebrows furrowed. "What happened to your father?"

She shrugged. "I don't know. I never spoke to him again and I've never gone back to that town."

He stared down at her for a long moment before he looked away, biting his bottom lip as he stared off into space. "Did he rape you, Nora?" he finally asked.

"No. He never penetrated me," she whispered.

Nodding, he looked down at her, his eyes almost black. "I'm going to kill him."

Her breath caught in her throat and her first thought was to tell him not to, to leave it alone, but she knew Angel wouldn't. He would hunt her father down and make him pay for hurting her. And somehow, that made her care about Angel even more. He hadn't been able to protect her as a child, but it was obvious he was going to go out of his way to protect her now.

"This is why talking is so hard for you. You're afraid to speak."

She nodded, lowering her eyes from his. "I don't know if I'll ever be normal, Angel. It's so ingrained in me. I'm too fucked up inside. You'd be better off finding someone else."

Tightening his arms around her, he shook his head. "I

don't give a fuck if you never speak, baby girl. I'll learn sign language. We'll text. I'll write you letters. We will figure out how to communicate. You're mine and I'm never letting you go. But I want to make one thing clear to you. I will never, ever, be angry at you for talking to me. I will never be angry at you for voicing your opinion, for standing up for yourself, for asking questions, or anything else that you say. It will take time but one day, I hope you will understand that you are safe with me. I will never hurt you, Nora. Never."

Tears started falling again. How he could declare something like that so early, she had no idea, but what she did know was that she believed it. She believed him.

Angel reached down and gently wiped her tears, taking special care on the side of her face that had the bruise. "Thank you for trusting me enough to tell me your past, baby girl."

She nodded and gave him a sad smile. "Thank you for sharing your past with me, too. I guess we're both kind of messed up, huh?"

A grin spread across his face as he nodded. "Yes, baby girl. But like I told you before, normal is boring. Besides, this means I get to be the one to show you just how wonderful and amazing life can be."

They stared at each other for a long time. Nora was emotionally drained and Angel looked like he felt the same.

Finally, he let out a sigh. "I didn't expect this morning to be quite so exhausting so how about after breakfast, we have some fun? You can have some Little time. Some stuff should have been delivered this morning to help you with that."

Little time sounded wonderful. It sounded like exactly what she needed.

"But what about you? It won't be fun for you to watch me play."

He chuckled. "Oh, baby, watching you play and be Little will be the most fun thing for me to do. Besides, it means I get to Daddy you a little bit. That is, if you're okay with that?"

Was she okay with that? Of course, she was okay with that. Especially if him Daddying her was anything like what he'd been doing with her the past few days.

"I think I'd like that," she murmured.

Angel led her downstairs, his hand wrapped firmly around hers. She felt so safe around him. It felt as if nothing bad could happen to her as long as he was around. He'd gotten dressed, but she was still in her pajamas. She'd pretty much been living in her PJs whenever they were at the house but she felt comfortable in them and every time she mentioned getting dressed, Angel reassured her that she was perfectly fine how she was as long as she was comfortable. The man always seemed to be looking out for her best interest.

She'd read hundreds of romance books over the years — it had been her only escape from her real life— and in those books the characters often fell in love with each other quickly. She'd thought for sure that stuff couldn't actually happen in real life but she was starting to second guess herself. She was falling for Angel and it didn't feel like a slow fall. No, it was a lightning speed fall.

"Since we already had pancakes last night, how about omelets for breakfast?"

Nodding, she smiled at him. "Sounds yummy. I can make them."

Furrowing his eyebrows, Angel turned to her as they stood in the kitchen and without warning, grabbed hold of her hips and lifted her so she was sitting on the counter.

Being that high up, she was at eye-level with him as he placed his hands on either side of the counter, crowding her space completely. She wasn't scared, though. Surprisingly. She was actually completely turned on.

"Let's get one thing straight, Little girl. In this relationship, I'm your caretaker. You might be the Little one and the submissive one but I'm the one who takes care of you. So that means when we're together, Daddy cooks, Daddy bathes you, Daddy cleans up, and anything else that needs to be done, Daddy takes care of. There will be times, when you're not in Little Space, that maybe you help me cook or you help me clean, but most of the time, I want to take care of you. Do you know what your job is?"

Well, if she didn't have to cook and clean and all the other things she was used to doing to try to appease Trevor, she would have a lot of free time on her hands to... do what? Be Little? Play? Read? Have fun? Huh. That sounded pretty good to her. But how would that be any fun for him? Wasn't she supposed to serve him since she was the bottom? This was all so new and different than what she'd experienced with her ex. Maybe she'd never truly gotten to experience what being Little was actually supposed to be like.

"But what do you get out of it? Taking care of me all the time would get tiring and it wouldn't be any fun for you."

Angel smiled and leaned forward, pressing his forehead against hers. "I get to take care of you. I get to protect you and watch over you, make sure you're always safe and happy. That makes me happy. And if you want to play or read or whatever it is that you want to do that makes you feel Little and relaxed, I'll love watching every second of it because that's what pleases me."

Having him so close, touching her, breathing the same air, and having his scent lingering around them, she couldn't help but squirm. Her panties were probably drenched, and she couldn't stop herself from wrapping her arms around him and burying her head in the crook of his neck. Her safe place. The place she was starting to think of as home. She'd always thought home would be a place, but she was quickly realizing it wasn't a place. It was a feeling. A feeling she'd never had before and one she never wanted to let go of.

16

ANGEL

When Nora released him, they both stared at each other for several seconds before he took a step back. It seemed even in their silent gazes they were communicating with each other.

He was so damn proud of her for opening up to him. It had to have taken a lot of courage. Whether she knew it or not, she was a damn strong woman.

Hooking his index finger under her chin, he leaned forward and placed a soft kiss on her mouth. "How about you keep me company while I make breakfast? That can be your way of helping."

She smiled widely, her dimples showing. He loved when he got a glimpse of them because it seemed they only appeared when she was really happy about something.

Pulling out some eggs, veggies, and cheese, he started prepping for the omelets. "Can I ask you some questions about your Little side?"

He could feel Nora's eyes on him as he chopped up the veggies.

"Yes."

"How young is your Little?"

When she didn't answer right away, he looked up to find an expression of confusion on her face.

"What do you mean?"

"I mean, like, some Littles don't like using sippy cups, some do, some prefer bottles, some Littles wear diapers, some don't, some like to have full care, and some like to be a little more independent. Where do you fall in all of that?"

She brought her hand up to her mouth and started nibbling on her fingernail. Putting the knife down, he moved over to her and gently pulled her fingers away. "Baby girl, there is no wrong answer here. I won't be upset or disappointed no matter what you say. My goal as a Daddy is to give you what you need and desire and I promise you, I will love it no matter what because I will get to be the one in control and taking care of you."

He was aware that he'd been calling himself Daddy as if he were her Daddy already. In his mind he was so it just slipped out. She didn't seem overly bothered by it, though, so he took it as a good sign.

Nora stared at him as he stroked the hand he'd just pulled free from her mouth. Letting go of her, he went back to cutting up veggies, wanting to give her a little space and a moment to gather her thoughts.

"I like being really Little. When I was with Trevor, I wore diapers a lot. I also had a bottle," she said softly.

Nodding, he smiled. "You like being taken care of intimately."

She nodded. "I did. He did a good job at first and I really liked it. As things started getting bad, he wouldn't change me so I started getting rashes."

Flexing his jaw, Angel's knuckles turned white as he gripped the knife. That fucking bastard. Just one more reason he couldn't wait to find him. "You will never have to deal with anything like that again. If we are in a dynamic where you are my baby girl and diapers are a part of that, my job is to make sure you're being taken care of the right way. What he did was neglectful and abusive."

She kept her eyes on his and slowly nodded. "I know that now."

"I'll get some diapers and bottles. I'll order a bunch of stuff for you to try and see if you like it."

A pink hue rose to her cheeks and she looked away from him. "You say that as if I'll be here forever," she murmured.

He nodded. "That's because I plan for you to be here forever, baby girl. I'm not a man who takes relationships lightly. When we enter into a relationship, we won't be dating. You won't be my girlfriend. You will be my every-thing and more. You will be my woman and my Little girl."

She pulled her bottom lip between her teeth and didn't say anything, but he could see the sparkle in her eye. She liked the idea of being his and staying here forever. He liked it, too.

———

AFTER THEY ATE BREAKFAST, which he fed her, he went to grab the boxes of stuff that had been delivered earlier. Over the last few days, he'd been ordering stuff online to be delivered for her. Maybe it had been wishful thinking, but he'd rather be prepared to take care of her.

Bringing the boxes into the living room, he started opening them, pulling out the items one by one while Nora sat curled up on the couch nearby. When he pulled out a baby doll, she gasped, her eyes wide with excitement.

"A baby," she murmured.

Smiling at her, he nodded and started removing the

doll from the packaging. It became obvious to him that he wasn't moving fast enough because she was wiggling and bouncing with excitement, scooting closer to him until she was practically plastered to his side.

Angel chuckled and finally got the last part of the toy free before handing it over to her. She instantly hugged the doll to her chest and took in a deep breath. "She smells like baby powder."

She held the doll up for him to smell and she was right, it did smell like baby powder.

"I love that smell," she said as she continued to hug the doll.

He made a mental note to pick up some baby powder to use on Nora for whenever she was ready for him to diaper her. He knew sometimes it was particular smells or sounds or textures that helped someone fall into Little Space.

"I ordered some more clothes for her, too. They should be in one of these boxes."

Opening box after box, he unpackaged all the toys until the living room looked like Christmas morning. Nora looked more excited than he'd ever seen her and as she moved from toy to toy, he could see a glimpse of her Little as she started playing. It didn't take long before she was lying on the floor on her tummy while playing with her toys. It was adorable and it seemed to be just what was needed after their draining morning.

The sound of Nora's giggles and the sight of her smiling face were enough to make his heart melt. She was perfect. Maybe not actually perfect. Perfection was an illusion. But she was perfect for him in every way.

The next several hours were spent with her playing and him watching. While he watched, he pulled out his phone and sent a group text.

Angel: I need a meeting. Can we meet at the gym tomorrow at ten?

Knox: Sure thing.

Hawk: Yep.

Beau: Yep.

Colt: I'll be there.

One by one, his brothers responded, confirming their meeting. It had been a long time since Angel had gotten the pleasure of hurting someone who hurt his family but now, not only was he going to get to hurt Trevor, he was also going to hunt down Nora's dad and make him pay. The motherfucker would die a very slow and painful death. Angel wasn't usually one to enjoy torturing people. He preferred to get the deed done and make the bad guys go away forever but this time... this time he was going to enjoy it. Relish every second of it. And once those two assholes were dead, he was going to walk away with a smile on his face.

He made her take a break to eat lunch and when she looked like she was about ready to cry because she had to leave her baby doll, he'd caved and told her to bring it to the table with her to join them for lunch. The look on her face was all he needed to see to know he'd done the right thing and when she passed him to go to the dining table, she stopped and wrapped her arms around his waist for a brief hug.

He might be a tough guy, but he had a feeling that with her he would be a complete pile of mush. But after all the shit she'd been through, she needed a Daddy who could be gentle with her.

When his phone started ringing after they finished

dinner, he tensed when he saw Colt's name on the screen. He hoped his brother finally had something on Trevor fucking whoever the fuck he was.

"Yeah?"

"Hey, man. Guess who showed up at Declan's safehouse?"

Turning to look at Nora, who was still on the floor playing, Angel walked down the hall to his office and sat down at his desk. "They got him?"

Colt sighed. "Unfortunately, no. The same car showed up there, but he only stopped briefly. He didn't get out of the car. Declan has men sitting at that house and we're hoping maybe he'll come back after nightfall. They'll be ready if he does."

"Okay. Thanks for letting me know. I need you to look at something else for me."

"Sure, what's up?"

Angel leaned back in his chair. "I need you to look up her father. I need to know his address."

Colt was silent for a moment before he asked, "Okay. Why?"

"Because I'm going to make him pay for hurting my Little girl. There's more than just one monster to find."

"On it. I'll send you the details when I find it."

"Thanks. I'll see you tomorrow at the gym."

When he hung up the phone and looked up, Nora was standing in the doorway with her stuffed hippo in her arms, looking a bit unsure.

He motioned for her to come in. "Come here, baby girl."

She stepped into the room, moving to him slowly as though she didn't want to make any noise with her footsteps. When she was close enough to him, he reached out and gently pulled her onto his lap. Her wrist was mostly healed but he didn't want to take any chances of hurting her.

His cock hardened as she wiggled on his lap, and he had to put his hands on her hips to still her before it became obvious to her. She looked at him with an alarmed expression.

"What are you doing, baby girl? All done playing?"

Lowering her gaze to his shirt, she twisted her fingers in it. "It's silly but I missed you when you were gone."

Smiling, he ran his hand up her back. "It's not silly. I missed you, too."

He leaned in and kissed her forehead lightly, then ran his fingers through her hair until she relaxed in his arms. Her fingers stroked his chest and his cock thickened. No matter how much he told it to chill out, the damn thing wouldn't listen.

Nora wiggled again, a small gasp escaping her lips, and he knew she'd felt it poking her bottom.

"Sorry, baby girl. I can control a lot of things but unfortunately, I can't control that."

She let out a soft giggle. "You don't have to be sorry. I... I kind of like knowing that it likes me."

"I think it more than likes you, baby girl. It hasn't been soft since the second I met you."

"Oh."

He leaned back in the chair staring at her while she stared back at him, her cheeks bright pink. When she wiggled her hips again, he groaned, making a slow smile spread on her face.

"You're teasing Daddy," he murmured.

She lowered her gaze. "Sorry. I'll stop."

Capturing her chin in his hand, she was forced to look at him and he shook his head. "Don't even think about stopping. I'm going slow because I don't want to scare you."

It felt as though there was a sizzle of electricity in the air between them as she nibbled on her plump bottom lip.

"You're not scaring me," she said quietly, her fingers splayed out on his chest.

Groaning, Angel moved his hand from her chin and let it slide slowly down her neck, stroking the pulse point with his thumb before gliding it a bit lower until he ran his fingers over her pebbled nipple. Their eyes locked and her mouth opened slightly as her breathing turned shallow.

Running the tip of his finger around her nipple, he teased it before moving over to the other one. She let out a soft moan, her hand gripping his shirt.

He was torturing himself, but he couldn't stop from touching her and even if they stopped right now, he knew it was still progress in the right direction. He just might have blue balls for a while.

Her green eyes stayed on his. She didn't seem scared, and he was pretty sure the occasional tremble of her body wasn't because she was cold.

"Baby girl, I need you to tell me to stop."

Another moan as he brushed his thumb over the peak of her nipple. Those damn moans of hers. It was like angels singing in the breeze. Angelic and sweet but also seductive.

"I don't want to," she whispered.

Dammit. He was so fucked.

17

NORA

"When was the last time someone gave you pleasure, baby girl?"

His dark, brooding eyes were fixed on her now, full of pure hunger, and she felt herself trembling under his touch. Nerves and arousal practically had her entire body buzzing with need. How could it feel so good just to have her nipples stroked? "Never, I guess."

Furrowing his eyebrows, he looked confused. "What do you mean never? Trevor never pleasured you?"

Yeah, right. That was a joke. The only one who got pleasure in their relationship had been him. She was pretty sure he wouldn't have been able to find her clit if there had been a bullseye right on it with flashing lights that said "It's right here."

"No," she whispered.

"You've never had a man strip you naked and spread your beautiful body out and make you scream using just his tongue?"

Shit. Her panties were soaked now and she was pretty sure she was only about thirty seconds from an orgasm with just his words alone. He'd said she needed him to stop but there was no way in hell she was putting a stop to this. Never in her whole life had she felt this close with someone and she didn't want to stop it. She wanted this. Whatever he would give her.

Slowly, she shook her head. "No."

His eyes darkened even more. "Has anyone ever given you an orgasm before, baby?"

Another head shake. If he was surprised, he didn't look it. No, the look on his face was pure possessiveness.

He stood suddenly and before she realized what was happening, she was in his arms being carried through the house.

"Where are you taking me?"

"I'm taking you up to my room where I'm going to strip you naked and lick and kiss and play with every inch of your beautiful body until you're begging me to stop giving you orgasms."

Whoa. She hadn't been expecting that. And she also wasn't scared, which said a lot. Even after she'd talked to Trevor for months, she'd been terrified the first time they'd gotten intimate. Yet another red flag she'd missed.

"If you want me to stop at any time, you just say stop or red. We will go over limits and boundaries another time but for now, if I do anything you don't like, you say either of those words. Understand?"

Meeting his dark eyes, she nodded.

"Words, Little girl. I won't force you to talk most of the time, but I need your words that you understand what I just said."

"I understand," she answered quietly.

As soon as he stepped into his bedroom, it felt as though the air between them changed. He kicked the door closed and set her on the bed, then leaned down and placed his hands on each side of her, his face level with hers. "Are you shaking because you're afraid or because you're turned on?"

Shit. She was shaking. And he wanted her to tell him why? She could feel her cheeks turn pink as she tried to think of an answer, but instead of making something up, she told him the truth. "A little of both. Not because I think you'd hurt me."

He kissed the tip of her nose. "You never need to be afraid of me. One thing you need to understand, Little one, is that even when we decide to make this official and I make you mine, you will be the one holding all the cards. You will draw the lines, and I will stay in those lines. I might be the Daddy, but you're the queen and the queen always rules the hive. Do you understand?"

She nodded and sucked in a breath. He shifted closer to her, his lips touching hers with feather-like caresses. As she sighed, he deepened the kiss just slightly, and she reached up, snaking her arms around his neck. She didn't have much experience with men— hardly any for that matter— but his kiss felt like so much more than just a kiss. His mouth coaxed hers open, and their tongues explored each other's.

Without even realizing it, she was kissing him back and moaning into his mouth. Something about him made her feel... free. Like she didn't have to hide. With Angel, she could just be.

When he released her mouth, she was panting. They stared into each other's eyes for a long moment before Angel rose to his full height and reached out, gently stroking her hair away from her face.

"I'm not very gentle sometimes, baby. I'll try to be gentle with you, but you might need to tell me if I'm being too rough. I don't want to hurt you, but I know that once I taste you, I'm going to be like a starving dog," he told her.

Holy wow. Angel was something else. A shock for sure. Different than anyone she'd ever met. He might be dark and brooding, but the fact that he wanted to be gentle with her touched her heart. She wasn't so sure she wanted gentle, though. It was so confusing because, while she didn't want the kind of treatment and abuse she'd gotten from Trevor, she also didn't want soft.

"Don't be gentle on me. Just please don't hurt me," she murmured.

His dark eyes turned black, and the expression on his face was so serious as he stroked her uninjured cheek with the back of his hand. "I'll never hurt you, baby."

Before she could say anything, he reached out and gently pushed on her shoulders so she fell back onto the bed with her legs dangling off the edge. He stepped in between her thighs, tucking his fingers into the waistband of her pajama bottoms. As he pulled them down, she watched as the muscles in his arms flexed. He was so muscular and sexy. His expression turned even more heated as he looked down at her panties. "You wore the panties I bought for you."

She nodded, suddenly feeling a bit shy. He was staring down at her cloth covered pussy, but she knew he could see her jiggly thighs, too. His gaze roamed down her legs and his heated expression turned to primal hunger as he dropped to his knees at the edge of the bed.

"Your body is perfection, Nora. I can see you having thoughts and I know I wouldn't like them if I knew what they were, would I?"

How did he know? How was it possible for him to read her like that? Was he that in tune with her? "No."

Bringing his hands up to her thighs, he squeezed them,

and she was shocked to see how much of her skin his large hands covered. Then she wondered how they would feel smacking her bottom.

"These beautiful legs of yours I'm going to love worshipping. Fuck, they're beautiful. Every part of you is beautiful. Your full bottom, your soft tummy, your big, beautiful tits. And that beautiful face of yours. I'll never get enough of it."

She whimpered and, when he lowered his face to her pussy and took in a long inhale, she moaned. He was smelling her through her panties. How was that so damn hot?

"I'm going to get you more panties like these. They look so fucking adorable on you," he said as he peeled them down.

Thank god she'd shaved her pussy the night before in the shower. She'd always hated hair down there so she kept it shaved at all times. He seemed pleased with it, too, as he stared.

"Fuck, baby. You please me. Your pussy lips are gleaming with your juices. I don't know if that's because of me or if it's because you've been neglected for so long but either way, I'm going to make you feel so good."

He didn't know if it was because of him? Was he high? Of course, it was because of him. Her pussy had been practically dripping since they'd met.

Before she could tell him that, he lowered his mouth to her and licked all along her lips, his tongue brushing against her clit just enough to make her head fall back against the mattress as she let out a low moan. Holy fuck! Should she be seeing stars already?

Whatever she should or shouldn't be seeing or feeling already didn't matter because she was, and she had a feeling there was no way to stop it from happening. He was a hard person not to feel things for. She just hoped it wouldn't be the biggest mistake of her life.

"What do you say if you want me to stop?" he asked, his eyes looking up at her.

"Red."

"Good girl. You're so beautiful. You smell like honey."

He darted his tongue out and swirled it around her clit, causing her to jerk and moan as he hit that perfect spot. She watched him as he lay between her thighs, his eyes locked on hers as he licked and sucked her clit. Moving his arms, he looped them under her knees and pushed her legs back so they were high and spread wide, and she knew everything was exposed to him down there.

Letting her head fall back onto the mattress, she moaned and whimpered as he ate her like she was his last meal. He wasn't just doing this for her pleasure. It was obvious by the way he was going at it that this was turning him on, too.

Gripping the bedding, she arched her chest up as her body started to tense up. Angel sucked on her clit harder, biting down on it with just enough pressure to make her scream out as an orgasm crashed through her. She thrashed and cried out, trying to close her legs to get away from the intensity but he held her tightly, continuing to play her body like an instrument.

"Angel," she cried out.

"That's a good girl, baby. Such a good girl," he crooned before lowering his head again.

Her head snapped up and she looked down at him as he started licking and sucking all over again, this time bringing his fingers to her pussy. He'd just given her the most amazingly, earth-shattering orgasm and he expected her to have another one?

"Angel, I can't."

"Mmm. You can, Little girl. You're going to. Be a good Little girl for Daddy and come all over my mouth again."

Oh, god. She felt one of his fingers at her entrance, massaging around her lips before slowly pressing inside of her. Sliding his other hand up her body, Angel slid up under her shirt and ran his fingers over her swollen nipples, teasing them and occasionally giving them a sharp pinch that had her crying out. The mix of pleasure and pain, between his strokes and licks to his pinches and bites, was the perfect balance that had her body tensing again.

He must have felt it because suddenly the finger inside of her curled up and stroked a spot inside of her she hadn't thought was a real thing. Holy fuck, it definitely was a real thing. It only took a couple of strokes before she was screaming again, hitting her hand on the mattress as her orgasm shot through her entire body, causing her legs to shake violently against his shoulders.

As she came down from the high, she'd expected Angel to pull away from her and be done but he continued to lap at her pussy with gentle licks, cleaning her up and groaning as he did.

"Angel," she moaned.

"Again, baby girl. I want to see you do that again," he growled.

Shaking her head, she reached for him. "I can't. I can't do it again."

The only response she got from him was a wicked smile as he continued toying with her nipples, his finger still deep inside her. It only took a few strokes on that delicate spot before she was panting again, squirming and bucking her hips against his hand. She was practically fucking his hand but instead of being embarrassed about it, she felt free and naughty and so damn sexy.

Angel lifted his head, watching her as he added a

second finger to her core. His fingers were so thick, she could feel them stretching her. She'd seen the outline of his erection through his pants and was pretty sure he was quite a bit bigger than his two fingers. She wondered how it would feel to have his cock inside her, stretching her even more. The thought made her cry out and he thrust his fingers in and out of her harder until she was practically levitating off the bed.

This orgasm lasted longer than the other two and she knew Angel was watching her the entire time because his mouth wasn't on her pussy. When she finally opened her eyes, he was staring at her with pure, animalistic hunger.

As her explosion subsided, she collapsed onto the bed feeling like jelly. Angel chuckled as he slowly and gently pulled his fingers from her. Peering at him from under her lashes, she watched as he licked his fingers clean, moaning as he did so, and holy hell that was a hot sight to watch.

Suddenly, she realized she needed to make him feel good, too. Sitting up, she bit her bottom lip as he stood and adjusted his erection. She looked up at him nervously, unsure of what to do, but he just shook his head.

"No, baby girl. That was purely for you. We aren't doing anything else today. I just wanted to make you feel good."

Confused, she furrowed her eyebrows. Why would he just want to make her feel good and get nothing in return? "But, I need to repay the favor."

His eyes darkened as he moved toward her. He got onto the bed next to her and cupped her chin. "You don't need to repay anything. It wasn't a favor. It was something I wanted to do to make you feel good and in return, it makes me feel good. There is nothing to repay. Once you're mine, there will be lots of times I just want to eat your pussy for my enjoyment. There will also be times that I want you to suck my cock for my enjoyment as long as that isn't a limit for you. But there will be no score to keep. Okay?"

Letting out a relieved sigh, she nodded. "Yes. I'm just not used to someone wanting to do things to make me feel good. And that felt... really, really good."

The look on his face changed into a grin as he winked at her. "Then I did it right."

She giggled and shook her head. Angel was such a different species of man. Of course, she only had two other men to compare him to and those two men had been monsters. She was starting to wonder if most men in the world were more like Angel and his brothers and she'd just been unlucky enough to meet two of the most horrible ones.

"And you're going to get used to someone doing things for you just to make you feel good because I'm going to love spoiling you. Especially since you've never been spoiled before," he told her as he leaned down and ran his lips over the shell of her ear.

Well, she couldn't exactly argue with that. Being spoiled sounded nice. Hell, she already felt spoiled with him. She also felt herself falling in love with him. It was both a terrifying and exciting thought.

18

ANGEL

"Why are we going to the gym?"

He eyed her as he helped her into one of his hoodies. It practically went down to her knees but seeing her in his clothes made his possessive side go wild. "Because I need to have a meeting with my brothers. There will probably be at least one of the other Little girls there."

Letting out a nervous sigh, she nodded. "Okay."

Two of Declan's men were at the door waiting for them when they walked out of the house. Angel knew Nora was intimidated by them. Their guns were visible in their waistbands. Angel was armed, too, though he always was when he left the house. It was just something that was ingrained in him after so many years of working in the shadows. They always needed to be prepared for anything.

Angel buckled her into the back seat of the black SUV before climbing in next to her and wrapping his arm around her shoulders. Something had shifted between them since they'd told each other about their childhoods. They were closer and she seemed even less afraid of him.

After he'd feasted on her pussy and cuddled her for hours the day before, he'd given her a bath. She hadn't argued but he could tell she felt unsure about him seeing her whole body. Normally he would have told her not to cover herself, but Nora was a different kind of Little. She needed someone who could handle her gently and while Angel had never considered himself a gentle man, he would try to be for her.

The gym was full of regulars as they walked in. Almost all the men who came to The Cage had been members for a long time and had come to the underground fights over the years. Because Angel and his brothers all spent so much time there working out, they knew almost everyone who came regularly. It was a safe place. Despite that, the people who came to work out there on a regular basis didn't know about the business they did in the back of the gym, so Angel instructed Declan's men to stay with the SUV and wait. They would be safe inside The Cage. There were no doubt a dozen or more men who would defend Angel and his brothers in the event there was trouble while they were there.

Lifting her out of the SUV, he took her hand and led her inside, nodding to several people he knew. Emma was standing at the front counter with another employee.

"Hey!" Emma called out excitedly, waving at Nora.

Nora's grip tightened on his hand, but she smiled shyly and waved back at Emma. "Hi."

"Beau is in the back room. Can Nora hang out here with me?" Emma asked.

Angel hesitated and looked down at Nora, who was smiling up at him with a hopeful expression. She looked like she wanted to stay and hang out with Emma, which surprised him, but he also took it as a sign that his baby girl was wanting to make more friends and he just couldn't say no to that. He really didn't want her right in the front of the gym, though. "Why don't you two go into the small gym and visit?"

There was a room in the gym that was smaller and had several punching bags set up for people who just wanted to get a workout in without sparring in a ring. It was also closer to the back of the gym where he would be.

Emma nodded and skipped around to where they were, taking hold of Nora's other hand. "Come on, Nora. We can go gossip about Angel."

Angel narrowed his eyes at Emma, making Nora giggle. Emma was becoming more and more naughty by the day. He still loved her dearly, but he was really going to have to talk with Beau about spanking her ass more. "No gossiping."

Shrugging her shoulders, Emma pulled Nora away from him and when he saw the girls disappear into the small gym, he made his way to the secure room where the men would be meeting.

His brothers were already there and when he walked in, they all stopped talking and looked at him expectantly.

"Where's Nora?" Wolf asked.

Wolf was such a funny creature. He was rough and tough and would slice someone's throat without even a wince but when it came to the Littles, he was the biggest fucking weenie there was. It was one of the most endearing things about his brother.

"She's in the small gym with Emma. They're gossiping apparently," Angel told them, rolling his eyes.

Beau smirked. "Afraid Emma is going to tell Nora all your secrets?"

Narrowing his eyes at his brother, Angel shook his head. "When it comes to Nora, I have no secrets."

His brothers all started laughing.

"Told you when you found your Little you would be helpless against her," Hawk told him.

Giving them all the finger, Angel sat down, shaking his head. Those fuckers could be so damn annoying sometimes.

"So, what was so important we needed to meet?" Beau asked.

Angel looked over at Hawk. "Has Ellie told you about Nora's past?"

Hawk furrowed his eyebrows and shook his head. "No. She's mentioned it was rough, but she didn't go into specifics. Why?"

Taking a deep breath, Angel tried to tamp down the anger that was bubbling within. "She was physically and sexually abused by her father her entire life. Like, daily. Ellie didn't find out until they were seventeen. That's why Nora is so quiet. She's terrified of talking for fear she might get hit. Even when she was little, she got beaten every time she spoke. Her father told people she was autistic and they fucking believed him because he's a goddamn doctor. That's why she was so afraid of Tate."

The room went silent as his brothers all stared at him with shocked and angry expressions on their faces. Hawk stood and started pacing, running a hand over his head as he let out a string of curse words.

"Who the fuck would do such a thing to their child? To any child? Motherfucking bastard," Wolf snapped.

"Colt, have you had any luck finding her father?" Angel asked.

Colt nodded. "I have. He still lives in the same town in the same house. He's still the resident doctor and has recently won awards for his work."

Angel crossed his arms over his chest and sat back. "Yeah, well, I hope those awards give him comfort over the next few nights because his days are numbered— and the numbers are small."

Knox nodded. "Whatever you need from us, you know we're here. Nora is family now and we're going to take care of her and protect her."

Nodding, Angel smiled at his brothers. They all got on his nerves sometimes, but he was one lucky son of a bitch to have them.

Suddenly, Emma came bursting through the door, her eyes wide, and everyone stood.

"What's wrong?" Angel demanded.

She looked around the room as if looking for something but then looked up at Angel. "I don't know where Nora is. She went potty and when she didn't come back a few minutes later I went to check on her, but she wasn't in the bathroom."

At once, the men dashed from the room with Beau instructing Emma to stay behind in the locked room. Angel rushed out front, looking around while the rest of his brothers spread out in search of Nora. Declan's men were outside keeping an eye on the building. They would have surely seen her walk out the front doors and let Angel know if that had been the case, so she had to be inside the gym somewhere.

Angel looked left and right, walking around all the cages and nodding to some of the members he knew. He didn't want to start any kind of alarm in the gym yet, so he stayed silent as he searched.

"Hey, man," one of the members said.

Looking at the man, Angel nodded. He recognized the guy but couldn't remember his name. He'd been a regular member of the gym for a couple of years but it had been months since Angel had seen him last.

"Hey," he replied quickly.

"I need to have a training session with you soon. I hear you're the one to go to for training."

Angel gave him a sharp nod as he continued looking around. "Sure. What was your name?"

"I go by Stone."

Directing his eyes toward the man, Angel had to bite back the laugh he was feeling. Stone? The guy was definitely not built like a stone. In fact, for being a member of the gym, he was pretty fucking puny.

"Anyway, I was hoping to train today but work called so I gotta take off," Stone told him.

Nodding, Angel walked past him and headed toward the back of the gym. It was obvious she wasn't out front. His brothers were still looking and Angel was really starting to panic. Where was his Little girl? Fuck!

"Nora!" he called out.

Nothing.

He walked into another room that held extra gear. "Nora!"

Nothing.

Fuck.

Walking into another room that had cleaning supplies, he looked around. "Nora?"

Sniffle.

"Nora! Fuck, baby, where are you?"

He started throwing stuff around trying to find her and when he caught a glimpse of her foot poking out from behind a trash can, he quickly moved it out of the way. She was curled up into a tiny ball, crying and trembling. Kneeling in front of her, he grabbed her and pulled her against his body, holding her tightly. "Baby, fuck, you scared me. What's wrong? Did you get lost?"

She shook her head and let out a sob. "He's here."

Everything in his body turned ice cold as he pulled her

away from his chest and looked down at her. "Who's here? Who?"

Tears spilled down her cheeks and she was shaking like crazy. It was scaring him how badly she was shaking.

"Trevor," she whispered.

Reaching back, Angel pulled his gun from the waistband of his pants and stood, looking around. He went to the door and opened it. "Knox! Beau! Any of you!"

The sounds of feet pounding the ground could be heard as Knox, Wolf, Hawk, and Beau all ran toward him.

"Lock down the gym. Trevor is here," he snapped before looking back at Nora. "What does he look like, baby? What is he wearing?"

She shivered. "He had on a red hoodie."

A red hoodie. Motherfucker!

His brothers had their guns pulled free and immediately went in search of Trevor while Angel went back to Nora. "Baby, I need you to come with me. I need to get you in a secured room."

Taking the hand he offered, she stood, and he could see her leggings were wet down her legs. She'd had an accident because of that bastard. Oh, that fucking guy was going to die. Stone. How many fucking names did this guy have? And what the fuck was he doing at The Cage?

Angel took her into the same room where Beau had left Emma and as soon as they were inside, Emma practically flew across the room when she saw Nora and hugged her. "Oh my gosh, I was so scared. Are you okay? Oh, what happened?"

"Emma, you and Nora need to stay in here. Can you help Nora out of her leggings and panties? The hoodie is long enough for her to wear for now."

Emma immediately nodded and Angel pressed one last kiss to Nora's head before he left the room and went to search for the bastard who hurt his girl. The gym was cleared out by the time he got out to the front and when Beau saw him coming, his brother shook his head. Fuck. He was gone.

"We've searched top to bottom. One of the older regulars said he saw a guy with a red hoodie walk out just a few minutes ago," Beau told him.

Clenching his fist, Angel slammed it into the wall, breaking the drywall. "Fuck!"

His brothers crowded around and they all stood in silence for a moment. "Let's lock up the gym for the day. We need to look at video footage to see who it is," Beau told them.

"I fucking ran in to him while I was looking for Nora. He said his name was Stone. I've seen him here before but not lately," Angel explained.

Beau furrowed his eyebrows. "Stone? Tall guy, kind of skinny with a buzz cut?"

Angel nodded. "Yep. Fuck, I need to go take care of Nora. She got so scared she had an accident."

"I have some spare clothes here for Emma, I'll bring you some stuff," Beau told him.

"Thanks."

Making his way back to the room where his Little girl was, Angel forced himself to ignore the rage he was feeling inside as he walked in, but the sight he found in the room only made it burn even hotter. She was on the floor with her knees pulled up and Emma's arms wrapped around her while she cried.

Walking up to them, he got down on the floor and pulled Nora into his arms, cradling her tightly. "Daddy's here, baby. I'm here. You're safe. I got you. Shh."

She cried for several minutes and when she finally

quieted, she looked up at him with a trembling bottom lip. "Did you get him?"

He shook his head. "He was gone before we got out there. We're going to review video footage and look up his membership record to see what we can find out. Did you know he worked out here?"

"No. He went to the gym sometimes, but he didn't say anything other than it was a gym. I assumed it was like a regular one. He didn't like when I asked questions."

Yeah, he didn't fucking like questions because he was up to something shady.

His brothers entered the room, keeping quiet as they walked around Angel and Nora on the floor. Emma ran into Beau's arms as he approached and clung to him. He picked her up and held out some clothes to Angel, who took them and started dressing her in the clean panties, making sure to keep the hoodie down so he didn't expose her to anyone in the room.

Her cheeks heated as she looked around and then back at him. "I'm so embarrassed."

Capturing her chin in his hand, he leaned forward and gently kissed her lips. "Don't be embarrassed, baby girl. These things happen. It's not your fault and no one is even blinking an eye about it. Their Littles have probably had accidents at times, too."

Once he had a dry pair of leggings on her, he stood and picked her up, settling her on his hip as he walked over to the chairs and sat down with her.

Colt was typing away on his computer. "This is the guy?" he asked, showing the screen to Angel and Nora.

She nodded and pointed. "That's him."

"Did he see you, baby?" Angel asked.

Shaking her head, she clung to his shirt. "No. I don't think so. I walked out of the room to find the bathroom and

I saw him out of the corner of my eye. As soon as I saw him, I took off running in the opposite direction."

He smiled down at her and kissed her forehead. "You did so well, baby. Such a brave and strong girl you are. I'm so proud of you for running. You did exactly what you should have done."

"Why was he here?" she asked.

Colt shook his head. "I don't know why the fuck he was here. He walked in, went to the locker room, came out for about two minutes, took a call, went back to the locker room, and then left."

Angel furrowed his eyebrows as he watched the video footage. "That bag he's carrying in. That's not the same bag he left with."

Colt replayed the video several more times. "No, it's not the same. Beau, do you have record of the last time he came?"

Beau nodded and set Emma beside him, pulling his own laptop onto his lap. "They sign in with a PIN number every time they come. Let me find his name from today and I'll look it up to see his sign in record."

It was complete silence in the room for several minutes while Beau searched and when he looked up, he glanced at Colt then Angel. "The name we have on file for him is Michael Sloan."

Angel looked down at Nora. "Have you ever heard that name when you've been around him before?"

She shook her head, her eyes wide. "No. Only Trevor Thomas."

Angel cursed. "He told me he goes by Stone. What the fuck is this bastard up to?"

"Here. I have his sign-in record. It's been sporadic over the last eight months though. He's only coming in like twice a month or so, usually a couple of days apart over the past few months. Before that he was coming a little more regularly," Beau said, showing the screen to Colt.

Colt started looking through video footage. "This might take a while. Why don't you take Nora home and I'll call you with updates. If anything, even if we don't even have this guy's real name on file, I can reach out to my friend, Ian, who has some pretty advanced software and see if he can use facial recognition to identify him."

Nodding, Angel wrapped Nora up in his arms and stood, carrying her with him as they all made their way out of the room. Declan's guys were posted inside the gym now and as soon as they saw them coming, they flanked Angel and Nora as they walked out to the waiting SUV.

19

NORA

She was mortified. Not only had she wet her pants, she'd run like a big baby and hid. And that stupid jerk got away. Why was he at the gym? That just didn't make sense. He'd never mentioned working out at an MMA gym. She had no idea he was into fighting. Well, she probably should have known but apparently, she was a big dumb dumbie who couldn't even see the giant red flags while they were waving right in front of her face.

Angel buckled her into the car and she couldn't even look him in the eye as he climbed in next to her. She was worthless and an embarrassment. What must his brothers be thinking? Angel was probably mortified. Keeping her eyes on her lap, she blinked back the threatening tears as Angel updated the men on what had happened.

When he was done talking, he turned to her. "Nora."

Instead of answering or looking up at him, she just shook her head, keeping her eyes pointed down.

"Nora, look at me."

She shook her head again, a tear rolling down her cheek.

"Baby girl, look at Daddy right now," he said in a low but firm voice.

Slowly, she raised her gaze to his and when he saw her face, his expression turned worried.

"Oh, baby girl. I'm so sorry we didn't get him. We will, though, I promise."

Nodding, she lowered her gaze but then his large hand reached out and captured her chin, tilting her head back so she was forced to look at him again. He studied her face for several seconds, his eyebrows drawn together. "What's going through your head, baby? Tell Daddy. I wish I could read your mind, but I can't."

She glanced over at the driver and the other man in the front seat, not wanting to talk in front of them. The last thing she wanted to do was cause Angel any more embarrassment by having these guys find out she'd wet herself. What kind of grown woman had accidents?

He must have realized that she didn't want to talk in front of the men because he released her chin and nodded, sitting back against the seat. "Okay, baby. When we get home, though, you're going to tell me what's going on in your head."

The rest of the ride to his house was silent but Angel kept an arm wrapped around her, stroking her arm the entire time. His warmth soothed her and she found herself slumping against him, unable to hold up her weight. How pathetic was she? She wasn't even strong enough to handle her own problems by herself.

As soon as they were parked, Angel got out of the SUV before reaching in and unbuckling her and pulling her into his arms. Instead of setting her on her feet, he carried her into the house and directly up the stairs, not stopping until they were in his bedroom. He set her down on the bed, placing his hands on either side of her hips as he squatted down until he was eye level with her.

"Tell Daddy what's going through that beautiful head of yours."

She shook her head. "Don't wanna."

His dark eyes felt as though they were piercing into her soul, making her squirm. He stared at her in silence for several seconds before he spoke again. "Why don't you wanna?"

Lowering her eyes from his, she felt her bottom lip tremble. "Because I embarrassed you. I'm so stupid and such a baby. I wet my pants. How pathetic am I?"

Surprise crossed his face and she flinched back without thinking, causing his eyes to widen.

"I'm sorry," she whimpered.

Angel lowered himself to his knees in front of her so he was now a few inches shorter than her as she sat on the tall bed. "Baby girl, I will never hurt you. Never. Oh, fuck, baby, I'm so sorry if I scared you."

Shaking her head, she swiped at the tears falling down. "You didn't scare me. I'm just so fucked up inside and I can't ever be normal, Angel."

He reached out and grabbed hold of both of her hands. "I don't like it when you say bad things about yourself so I'm giving you your first rule and it's going to be one of the most important. No more talking negatively about yourself. Enough people have hurt you in your lifetime and I'm not going to allow anyone else to ever hurt you again, and that includes you hurting yourself. So no more calling yourself names or putting yourself down. Are we clear on that?"

More tears fell down her cheeks but she couldn't help but nod.

"Secondly, I am not embarrassed about you. I will never be embarrassed about you. Having an accident is nothing to be embarrassed about. It happens, baby. It happens to lots of Littles. Nothing you do will ever make me embarrassed or ashamed of you."

She sniffled. His words were so forceful and genuine, she wanted to believe them. She felt as though he was telling her the truth. Angel wasn't the type of man to lie.

"You might be a baby, but you're my baby, Little girl. At least I want you to be. I want you to be mine. I want to take care of you and be your Daddy," he added.

She wanted him to be her Daddy, too. More than anything she'd ever wanted in her life.

"I want that, too," she murmured.

"Do you trust me enough to give me a chance?"

She didn't even have to think about it before she nodded. "Yes."

His lips pulled back into a wide smile that made her heart melt. Reaching up, he pulled her into his arms and held her tightly, pressing kisses into her neck.

"Look at me, Little girl," he told her. "I will never be embarrassed by you or anything you do. I will never put you down for an accident or make you feel less than perfect. One day you'll come to understand that when I'm able to take care of you in the most intimate ways, that's when I'm the happiest."

Letting him take care of her sounded so wonderful. Nodding again, she reached out and twisted her finger in his shirt. "I'm sorry I flinched," she whispered.

He stared up at her, his eyes searching before he shook his head. "Don't ever apologize for that, baby. I will try to be more careful. I never want to scare you."

"Please don't be careful with me. I don't want you to treat me differently than you would any other Little. I need to learn not to be so afraid. I don't want you to change who you are because of my problems."

Bringing his large hands to her thighs, he stroked them soothingly. "I will treat you differently no matter what because you aren't just any other Little, you are *my* Little, and that means your problems are now my problems and we will work through them together. You're no longer alone, baby."

Nodding, she leaned forward toward his chest and without any hesitation, he pulled her down into his arms and rolled back onto his butt on the floor, holding her close. "I got you, baby girl. I'm never letting you go."

She settled into his warmth and sighed, resting her head against his shoulder. It had been an exhausting day so far and all she wanted to do was submerse herself into Little Space and relax. As if he knew exactly what she needed, he shifted her so she was cradled in his arms like a baby as he stared down at her.

"I think the rest of today needs to be spent in Little Space and you need to let Daddy take care of you. You said you enjoyed wearing diapers and that's when you felt the most relaxed so if it's okay with you, I'd like to put you in a nice, thick diaper and some soft clothes for the rest of the day. Would that be okay with you?"

Her cheeks turned bright pink and she could feel the heat spreading over her body as she nodded. He'd already had his mouth on her most private parts so it wasn't like he would be seeing her naked for the first time. And even though she felt a little embarrassed about him taking care of her so intimately, she also really wanted it. "Uh huh."

The corners of his eyes crinkled as he smiled. "That's my good girl. I ordered several different kinds for you to pick from. They all have cute designs on them specially made for a cute Little girl."

Angel got to his feet with her still in his arms, then set her on the bed and handed her the stuffed hippo he'd given her. When she had it clutched to her chest, he held up the pacifier she'd used the night before and brought it up to her lips, sliding it in when she opened for him. She could tell he was pleased with that and it made her feel good to make him as happy as she felt.

"I'll be right back. Don't get off the bed by yourself. I don't want you to fall," he told her with a stern look before he disappeared into the walk-in closet.

A moment later he reappeared with several thick diapers in his hand and some clothing. When he came and stood before her, he held up the diapers, showing her each one. They were all different. One was plain white, while another was a light pink with flowers printed on the front, and a third had farm animals printed all over it.

"Which one, baby?"

She eyed them for several seconds before pointing to the pink one. She liked pink. It was a color that instantly made her feel Little. He nodded and winked at her. "Good choice."

He pulled off the hoodie she was still wearing and when he reached out and grabbed the hem of her shirt, she tensed slightly, but he slowly and carefully pulled the top over her head. Next, he reached behind her and unhooked the bra and pulled it down her arms, letting her heavy breasts hang free. She instantly covered them with her arms but when she looked up and met his gaze, all she saw was hunger in his eyes.

"I don't want you to hide from me, baby girl. I think your body is beautiful and sexy and it's going to be my own personal playground that I'll never get tired of playing with," he told her gently.

She liked that he wasn't overly forceful. She suspected he could be at times, but it seemed he knew when it was the right time to assert his dominance. Wanting to please him, though, she lowered her arms to her sides. He stared at her breasts for several seconds, licking his lips as he did so, and she felt herself tingling all over. Just the way he looked at her was enough to get a wildfire raging inside her body.

"Lie back so I can take your pants and panties off," he said, taking one of her hands in his to help her lower herself.

When she was flat on her back, he removed her shoes first before hooking his thumbs into the waistband of her leggings and panties, peeling them down her legs and leaving her completely naked before him. His gaze was pure hunger but he didn't act on it. Instead, he fluffed up the pink diaper and grabbed hold of both her ankles in one hand, raising them high so he could slide the diaper under her bottom.

She was surprised how quickly he had her wrapped securely into the diaper, as if he'd done it a million times. It was snug but not too tight and when she tried to close her legs, the thick, crinkly material didn't allow it.

Next, he held up what looked like a diaper cover. It was cotton and had ruffles around the leg holes. It was also lavender and had white polka dots on it. It was so cute and when he slid it up her legs and settled it over her diaper, she couldn't help but smile.

Angel reached out and gently grabbed hold of her hand, pulling her up to sitting. The diaper crinkled loudly as she moved, making her blush, but he didn't seem the least bit fazed by it as he lowered a long-sleeve lavender shirt over her head. On the front of the shirt was a purple hippo with a bow on its head. It was so cute she could hardly stand it. He'd ordered her clothes he knew she would like because of her favorite animal. It was just another reason why she knew her feelings for Angel were morphing into love. And she knew it would be a love that would kill her if it ever ended.

"You look adorable, baby. Come here," he said, lifting her from the bed and settling her on his hip.

He carried her into the bathroom, set her on her feet in front of the mirror, and stood behind her watching her reflection. Without saying anything, he grabbed her hairbrush and started combing through her tangled hair so gently she didn't feel it snag even once. It only took a few minutes before he had her long tresses pulled up in a high ponytail and a ribbon tied at the base of it.

She couldn't help but smile at her reflection. Her cheek was no longer swollen and the bruising was now a pale yellow color so it wasn't as easy to notice right away. As she stared at herself, the only thing she saw was a happy Little girl. A genuinely happy one at that.

"Thank you," she murmured.

Sliding an arm around her front, he pulled her back against his chest and tilted his head to kiss her on the cheek. "You're welcome, baby girl. You look as sweet as can be. How do you feel?"

Letting out a contented sigh, she smiled. "I feel Little."

A grin spread across his face. "Then we did it right. Now, it's time for my Little girl to play with some toys while her Daddy makes some lunch."

He took her hand and led her from the bathroom and with every step she took, the diaper crinkled, making her giggle. She'd never be able to hide from him and get away with it, that was for sure. Not that she would want to. There were a lot of people in the world she wanted to hide from forever, but Angel was not one of those people.

When they got downstairs, Angel took her to the living room and turned on an animated movie, then spread out a soft pink blanket on the carpeted floor. "Play, baby girl. I'll be right in the kitchen if you need me."

Nodding, she knelt down and immediately reached for the baby doll that he'd gotten her. It was definitely her favorite toy out of all of them but really, she loved everything.

Only a few minutes later, Angel walked into the living room with a pink plate and a pink bowl in his hands and sat down on the couch. He set the dishes on the coffee table and motioned for her to come to him. "Come here, baby girl."

Looking at her doll, she hesitated and then looked at him, shaking her head. She wasn't ready to stop playing yet. She'd only just started. Angel raised an eyebrow at her. "Little girl, come here. It's time for lunch. You can play with your toys after you're done eating."

Keeping her gaze on the doll, she tried to ignore him even though everything inside her was telling her to listen to him so he didn't get angry with her. She hadn't ever been defiant. It wasn't something she'd ever been brave enough to do because she knew what would happen to her if she was, but for some reason, with Angel, she wasn't afraid.

"Nora, Daddy is going to count to three and if you're not over here by the time I get to three, you and your dolly are going to spend ten minutes with your noses in the corner before lunch. One."

Her eyes widened and she looked up, meeting his stern gaze. He wasn't joking. Timeout sounded terrible. Absolutely boring. And it wasn't nice that her dolly would have to go to the corner, too.

"Two."

Letting out a squeak, she put her doll down and scrambled over to him. He smiled at her and nodded, patting his lap. "That's my good girl. Come here."

As she crawled onto his lap, she could feel his erection pressing into her bottom. She was starting to feel kind of bad. It seemed he was constantly walking around with a hard-on.

"Thank you for coming before I had to punish you," he told her.

He grabbed the plate of food and started feeding her bites of the sandwich that he'd cut the crust off of. Their eyes stayed focused on each other as he fed her, and it felt strangely intimate. She was starting to realize everything with Angel felt intimate.

The idea that he was her Daddy now was still so surreal but for the first time in her life, despite everything else that was going on, she felt truly happy all the way down to her bones.

20

ANGEL

God, could he get any luckier? Nora was the cutest baby girl he could have ever imagined, and she slipped into that headspace so easily. He could still see a little timidness in her, but he'd been shocked that she hadn't come right to him when he'd told her to come eat her lunch. He was also very proud of her. There was no doubt in his mind that she would never be the type of Little that brats all the time, but he did want her to get to a place where she felt safe enough to be naughty or break the rules.

Holding a piece of sandwich up to her mouth, he decided to try and get her talking. He wanted to learn her limits and things she did or did not want to experience in their relationship. He also needed to know what kind of discipline he could provide for her that would give her the security she needed in this kind of relationship without scaring her or causing harm.

"When you've thought about the perfect dynamic in your head, what kinds of things do you think of when it comes to consequences?"

She furrowed her eyebrows as she chewed her bite then swallowed. "Like punishments?"

He nodded and held up a sippy cup of water for her. She took it from him, seemingly deep in thought about his question as she took a drink.

"It's going to sound so stupid because of everything I went through growing up, but I've most often fantasized about being spanked. I know there must be something wrong with me because of that."

Shaking his head, he reached out and hooked his index finger under her chin, lowering his face so it was close to hers. "No saying negative things about yourself, Little girl. It's not stupid and there is nothing wrong with you. Being spanked is completely different than being abused. Two totally different things. One is controlled, consensual, and is something both people talked about and have agreed upon beforehand. The other is non-consensual and is abuse."

Biting her bottom lip, her sad green eyes looked into his. "It's not weird that I want to be hit? Even though I've been hit all my life?"

Angel shook his head, swallowing down the rage he was feeling for her father and her ex. They would pay dearly for hurting his Little girl.

"Baby, it's not weird. Nothing you want or need is weird. Never. If you told me you never wanted to be spanked, I would understand completely, but it's not weird if that's something that you want. A lot of submissives and Littles need to be spanked sometimes to help clear out all the icky stuff in their heads. Some need it because they need to experience the pain. And some need it for various other reasons. Okay?"

She nodded. "I wouldn't ever want to be spanked with a belt. Or a cord."

Swallowing the growl he felt, Angel took a steadying breath. "He hit you with a cord?"

Lowering her eyes from his, she nodded. "Yes. Usually his belt, but sometimes if he wasn't wearing one, he'd grab an extension cord or whatever kind of cord was close by."

Fuck. His poor little baby.

"I will never ever spank you with my belt or a cord. If I ever use an implement to spank you, we will discuss it first. You can say no to anything at any time and even if you agree to something and we try it and it ends up scaring you or hurting you more than you want, you'll always be able to use your safeword and it will stop immediately. Okay?"

"Okay."

"Good girl. So spankings. Bare bottom?"

She nodded. "I've always fantasized about it being bare bottom."

"Okay. What else? Timeout? Lines? Being grounded? Early bedtime? Are all those okay with you?"

"Yes, but they all sound very boring," she muttered, looking down at her lap.

He laughed and nodded. "Punishments aren't supposed to be fun, Little one. They are supposed to teach you a lesson. What about punishments you never want to happen? Anything you can think of?"

"I don't want you to scream at me. Or hit me in the face. Or lock me in a closet."

Tightening his arms around her, he buried his face in her neck and hugged her for several minutes before he could speak. The lump that had formed in his throat was so thick he had to swallow several times first. "I would never, never do any of those things. It doesn't matter what you do, Little girl, I would never do that to you."

She hugged him back and he could feel her shaky

breaths as she nodded her head against his shoulder. "Thank you."

How was it that this woman, this sweet and beautiful woman, could have ever been treated so badly? What kind of person was such a monster?

They sat in silence for a long time, hugging as he stroked his hand up and down her back. It seemed as though it was as much reassurance for her as it was for him.

When she started squirming in his lap, he pulled away and looked down at her. "What's wrong?"

A pink hue rose to her cheeks and she lowered her eyes from him. "I need to go potty."

Confusion filled him. "Okay. You have a diaper on, baby. It won't leak."

Her cheeks went from pink to bright red. "I can go on the toilet so you don't have to change me."

Oh, this Little girl had so much to learn about him.

"Or you could use your diaper and I can change you and take care of you because that's what I want to do. If you really don't want to use your diaper, I won't force you. We can always get you pull-ups so they're easier to get on and off when you use the toilet."

She shook her head. "I... I like using my diaper. It makes me feel so safe and Little. I just don't want to be a bother."

"Look at Daddy," he instructed. "You are never a bother, baby. I know this is still new but eventually you're going to understand that taking care of you, feeding you, bathing you, putting you to bed, changing your diaper, all those things are things I love doing. It gives me control and makes me feel good. You will never ever be a bother, even if I have to change your diaper every hour of every day. Okay?"

She nodded. "Do the other Littles wear diapers?"

"I think some more than others. I know Brynn is almost

always in diapers. Ellie is, too, quite a bit. I think Lucy, Addie, and Ava wear them sometimes and I think Kylie and Emma wear them at bedtime. I don't think Claire wears them at all. You know you can always reach out and ask them questions. I know you talk to Ellie, but all the girls are excited to become your friend. Even if you only feel comfortable texting with them."

Nora smiled and nodded. "I think I'd like to be their friend, too."

"You may not realize it yet, Little one, but you're part of this family already. You will have lots of Little friends and lots of overbearing, protective, yet loving uncles."

"Do you spank the other girls or change their diapers?" she asked quietly.

Was she jealous? Not that he minded. He kind of liked the idea of Nora being jealous of him possibly spanking or touching the other women.

"I have never spanked them or changed them. I've held them on my lap, I've bottle-fed a couple of them, and I've tucked some of them into bed before. All the Littles and Daddies have their own relationship rules. I know Kylie has been spanked by several of us brothers but only because that is something she and Ash agreed upon being allowed. I know Lucy has been spanked by a couple of them, too. And I know Brynn has had her diaper changed by a couple of my brothers. But none of these things happen without the consent of the Little and the Daddy in each relationship. So, if you told me you didn't want me to spank another one of the Littles or change their diapers or even let them sit on my lap, it would never happen, just like if you didn't want one of my brothers to spank you or change your diaper, it would never happen. Everything that happens in these relationships is consensual. Does that make sense?"

Nora nodded and he realized she was blushing.

"What are you blushing about, baby girl?"

She shrugged, biting her bottom lip, but Angel wasn't going to accept that for an answer. "Baby girl, the most important thing about our relationship is communication. If there is something you want or need out of it or are even interested in but not sure, I need you to communicate that with me so I know how to be the best man and Daddy I can be."

"But I don't want to hurt your feelings or say something that would upset you," she said quietly.

Raising his eyebrows, he tilted his head. "The only thing that would upset me or hurt my feelings is if you told me you didn't want to be with me. I will tell you I don't share and I never will, so if you want to have sex with another man, that would cause an issue because you're mine and I'm yours. But if there was something else you wanted to try or experience, I want to know about it."

She giggled and rolled her eyes. "I can promise you I will never want to have sex with another man."

He shrugged and grinned. "You haven't even had sex with me yet, so how can you know? I might have an itty-bitty teeny weenie for all you know."

She burst out laughing, her entire body shaking as she did, making him laugh right along with her.

"I've seen the outline of it and felt it press against my bottom. It's definitely not an itty-bitty teeny weenie," she said through her fit of laughter.

They continued to laugh for several minutes and when they both finally calmed down, he looked her in the eye. "Then what was making you blush?"

"I definitely don't think I would want anyone else to spank me. I've been hurt enough in my life that trusting you to spank me is probably all I can handle. But I don't know, the thought of having one of your brothers change my diaper or hold me on their lap or something, it's kind of hot. Not that I want to have sex with them or anything because I wouldn't want that. I think it just makes the dynamic of being Little feel so much more immersed when there is more than one person around you that will take care of you when needed. Maybe it's weird but I've read it in books before and I always thought it was so sweet and also kind of hot."

Angel nodded. "Thank you for being honest with me. I understand what you're saying, baby girl, and that's why all of us take care of the Littles in different ways up to their comfort level. It's okay to find it hot, as long as the only one who's making love to you is me. I know my brothers are good looking and are awesome Daddies and Uncles."

She nodded. "They all seem nice. I don't know if I'll ever have the guts to really talk to them, though."

"They can still look after you without you talking to them. Lots of baby girls go non-verbal when they are in that headspace. I know Brynn goes non-verbal often and we still take care of her."

Twisting her fingers in his shirt, she nodded. "I don't think it would bother me if you changed another Little's diaper or spanked them. I wouldn't want you to have sex with them or anything like that, though."

Leaning forward, he kissed her forehead. "The only person I will be having sex with for the rest of my life is you, Little girl. You will be the only person I fuck, lick, bite, and kiss. There will never ever be anyone else for me."

Her pupils dilated and her breathing turned shallow. She was getting turned on. He was turned on, too. Fuck, when hadn't he been turned on since he'd met her? But that wasn't what this afternoon was about. It was meant to be a day for her to relax and enjoy being Little. One thing would always hold true in their relationship; her needs would always come before his wants.

"Let's finish eating and then Daddy will take you up and change your diaper before naptime," he said, changing the subject.

She took the bite he was holding up to her mouth and chewed on it, moaning happily. His cock ached against his jeans. Maybe while she was napping, he'd take a very cold shower. He might even need an ice bath to get his cock to settle down.

"I will make sure my brothers are clear on the no spanking you boundary, and if it ever comes down to them changing your diaper, how about if I tell them it's okay, but if you ever tell them you'd prefer your Daddy to do it then they won't do it, okay?"

She thought about that for a moment before nodding. "Thank you, Daddy."

Angel froze, his eyes widening as he realized what she'd just called him. A lump formed in his throat and his chest tightened. It was the first time in his entire life that someone had called him Daddy, and it truly meant something to him.

Her eyes were wide, too, and her mouth dropped open into an O as if she'd just realized she'd called him that. Wrapping his hand around the back of her neck, he pulled her toward him and kissed her deeply. When she moaned into his mouth, he nearly exploded in his underwear. Pulling back, he smiled at her, their foreheads resting together.

"I love hearing that come out of your mouth."

She smiled sweetly. "I like saying it."

"Then never call me anything else again."

"What about in public?" she asked.

He shrugged, stroking his thumb over her jawline. "I don't care what anyone else thinks."

"Me either," she whispered.

"Good."

They stared at each other for several seconds with smiles spread across their faces.

"Okay, baby. Let's go get you ready for naptime."

"But, I'm not sleepy," she said through a yawn.

He shot her a look that made her giggle and he practically melted over the sweet sound. Picking her up, he settled her on his hip and made his way upstairs, leaving the dishes to deal with later.

When they were back in his bedroom, he set her down on his bed so she was resting on her back and pulled the diaper cover down. He quickly worked to change her wet diaper and replace it with a fresh one. Once that was done, he pulled the blankets back and patted the bed. "Come on, Little girl."

She crawled on all fours into her spot and settled under the blankets. Angel tucked her in and set the stuffed hippo in her arms before sliding her pacifier between her lips again. Leaning down, he kissed her forehead. "I want you to try to sleep. I have a baby monitor right here so if you need me just call out and I'll be right here. I need to go make some calls."

Letting out a sleepy sigh, she nodded and smiled at him behind the pacifier guard. He was pretty sure she was sound asleep before he even made it out of the bedroom.

———

ANGEL WENT DOWN to his office, carrying the other end of the baby monitor with him, and sat down at his desk. He hoped

Colt would have some information for him by now so they could find this fucker and figure out why he had been at the gym. Just the fact that he came with one gym bag and left with a different one meant he was doing something shady. Not that it was really a surprise; the guy seemed shadier than a forest.

"Hey," Colt answered.

"Find anything?"

Colt cleared his throat. "Actually, I think I have. I've been running through security footage at the gym since I got home and it seems as though Trevor always shows up with a bag and leaves with a different, fuller looking bag. So I kept looking through the footage and found another guy who shows up with the bag Trevor leaves with and the guy takes the empty looking bag that Trevor shows up with. They are doing some kind of transaction."

Fuck.

"Do we know who the guy is that is exchanging these bags?" Angel asked.

"Actually, we do. We've known him for many years. Luis Salvatore."

What the fuck? Luis Salvatore was someone they knew from the fighting circuit. He was a drug dealer who liked to bet on fights. He was also a member of the gym and worked out regularly. Angel had even done training sessions with him. They'd known him for years. The guy was in his fifties at least by now.

"We need to talk to him," Angel stated.

"Yeah. Beau is working on getting a meeting with him. We'll see how willing he is to talk, though. Pop said he'll watch the girls while we meet with him."

Angel nodded, unsure if he wanted to leave Nora with Pop. It wasn't that he didn't trust Pop, because he did. He trusted him more than anyone in the world, but it was Nora he worried about. She had only met him once and Angel didn't want to do anything to upset her or cause her to close up on him. But having her with Pop would be safer than having her with him at the meeting, even with Declan's men there.

"Beau just sent me a text and said Salvatore agreed to meet us at nine tonight at the warehouse."

Shit. There was no way Nora was going to the warehouse with them, even with Declan's men there for extra protection. His poor baby girl had already seen and experienced enough scary shit in her life. Going to a warehouse was not ever going to be on that list of things she'd experienced.

"Fuck. Okay. I need to call Pop and talk to him about watching her."

Colt grunted. "Okay. Let's plan on dropping the girls off at seven and meet at the gym around eight to make sure we have a plan."

"Yep."

After hanging up with Angel, he found Pop's name in his phone and called him.

"Hey, Pop."

"Hey. Beau just called me and said all of you are bringing the girls over tonight."

Angel sighed. "Yeah. About that. You know Nora is shy. She probably won't even speak to you when she's there."

"That's fine, son. You know I'll love her no matter what. I'll learn how to communicate with her in a way that makes her feel safe and comfortable."

This was why Angel knew he was so damn lucky. Pop didn't have to love and accept any of the guys except for Beau but both he and Ma did, and Pop had also welcomed every one of the Littles into their family as well. Angel just hoped Nora would come to understand how loved she was by not just him but his entire family. And she was loved by him. Immensely. He just needed to find the right time to tell her so he wouldn't scare her away.

"Thanks, Pop. She might be diapered when she comes."

"That's fine. You know I'll take care of her if she is. She'll be just fine, and I'll call you if anything comes up. Ellie will be here, too, so she can help me if I'm not sure about anything," Pop replied.

"Okay. Love you, Pop. Thank you... for everything. I know I wasn't easy."

Pop chuckled. "Angel, you went through pure hell as a kid. I would have been worried if you'd been an easy teenager. I hope you know how incredibly proud I am of you. You're a good man. I'm a damn lucky man to have you as my son."

Angel had to swallow several times to get the lump that was forming in his throat to go away. Pop was a tough man and didn't look like the type of man to share his feelings, but his looks were deceiving because there hadn't been a day that had gone by since Angel moved in with him that Pop hadn't told him he loved him and was proud of him.

"I'll see you later, Pop."

"Okay, son. See you later."

21

NORA

She didn't even have to open her eyes to know her Daddy was in the room with her. She could smell him and feel his presence, something that made her feel wonderfully safe and secure.

"Daddy," she whispered.

"Yes, baby girl. I'm right here."

Slowly opening her eyes, she found him sitting right beside the bed watching her. His dark eyes seemed to lighten as soon as she met them. How was it possible to already care so deeply for him? She knew the answer without even having to really think about it. He made her feel safer and more cared for than she'd ever felt in her entire life. He was also fine as hell with a good personality, which was just the icing on the cake.

"Did I sleep long?"

He smiled and leaned forward, reaching for her hand. "A couple of hours. It's nearly dinnertime. I didn't want to wake you, though. You need to rest as much as possible."

"How long have you been sitting here?"

"For about an hour."

"Oh." She felt a flush run through her body at the thought of him watching her sleep. Like a guardian angel or something. Was it weird she liked that he'd been watching her? It didn't feel weird.

He ran his thumb over the back of her knuckles. "I have a meeting tonight that I need to go to. You and the other girls will go to Pop's house while we're gone."

She tensed and she felt her eyes widen. Where did he have to go? Couldn't she go with him or stay at the house alone? Anything other than going to another man's house. "I can stay here. I promise I won't touch anything or snoop or anything. I'll sit on the couch the entire time and won't get into anything."

Angel shook his head as he reached for her, pulling her onto his lap. She was panicking inside and trying not to freak out outwardly.

"Baby girl, first of all, you can snoop and touch anything in this house you want because this is your house, too. I have nothing to hide from you. I don't care if you go through every single drawer in my bedroom or office. I will have no secrets from you. But you can't stay here alone. Not until we get rid of any possible threat. He's already been in this neighborhood once.

"I know you don't know Pop yet, but he won't ever hurt you, baby girl. None of the men in my family would ever hurt you. The other girls will be there, too, including Ellie, so at least you'll have someone familiar there. I need you to be brave for me so I can go into this meeting without worrying about if you're okay. Do you think you can do that for Daddy?"

Ugh. She couldn't say no to that. He wanted to take her to his Pop's place to keep her safe. He wasn't just doing it to do it. But Ellie would be there and she felt safe with Ellie. Maybe she could get to know the other Little girls a bit.

Hopefully Pop would just ignore her so she wouldn't embarrass herself or Angel when she couldn't even talk to him.

Taking a deep breath, she nodded. "Okay."

By the time Angel had packed her an overnight bag and they were in the black SUV to go to Pop's house, she was a bundle of nervous energy. Even though Pop's house was only at the end of the street, Angel and the bodyguards hadn't wanted to take the chance of walking, so she fidgeted during the entire thirty second drive. Ellie had texted her after she'd eaten dinner to say how excited she was to hang out, and Nora was looking forward to that.

She just hoped the other girls wouldn't think she was weird or treat her badly because of how shy she was. Both Ellie and Angel had assured her that no one would think anything negative about her or treat her badly, but she was so conditioned to that kind of thing that it was hard to really believe it.

Angel carried her right into Pop's house without knocking and as soon as they were inside, she could hear several women giggling. Setting her down on her feet, Angel took her hand and led her into the large open living room where Ellie and Lucy and several of the other Littles she'd met at the gym were sitting around the coffee table playing a board game.

Ellie immediately jumped up and ran over to them, throwing her arms around Nora. "I'm so glad you're here. I've been dying to see you."

Letting out a happy sigh, Nora hugged her best friend back. She was so glad she had someone familiar around her. Ellie had always been such a good friend, protecting her from bullies and making her feel part of things at school. "I missed you," Nora whispered in her ear.

Ellie gave her one more squeeze before releasing her then smiled widely up at Angel. "Hi, Uncle Angel."

"Hey, Little one. Are you being good for Pop?"

Shrugging, Ellie shook her head. "No."

Pop chuckled as he walked into the room. "Of course she is, because she knows if she's naughty I'll tell her Daddy and then she'll get her bottom spanked."

Nora couldn't stop herself from smiling. Ellie had always been a bit of a handful but that was one of the things Nora loved so much about her.

When Pop walked toward them, Nora stepped closer to Angel, trying to hide behind his arm. Angel tightened his hold on her hand and leaned down so his mouth was near her ear. "You're safe here, baby. No one will hurt you here."

His soft words instantly soothed her and she relaxed slightly as Pop got closer.

When he stopped a few feet shy of Angel and Nora, she glanced up at him from under her lashes. Leo was smiling kindly at her. "Hey, sweet girl."

She eyed him, unable to reply or even smile but it didn't seem to faze him. He didn't seem angry or annoyed that she didn't respond. Instead, he walked over to one of the end tables at the couch and opened the drawer, pulling something out before walking back over to them and kneeling in front of her.

"I heard that hippos are your favorite. They're one of my favorites, too. I found this when I was at the store earlier and had to get it for you. I figured if things are too loud or overwhelming tonight, you can take it to a quiet area and color in it," Leo said, holding out a coloring book with a big pink hippo on the front.

Biting her bottom lip, she looked up at Angel who was

smiling down at her. When their eyes met, he nodded. Lowering her eyes to Leo, she smiled softly and reached for the book he was holding out. He winked at her as he rose to his feet while she looked at the book. It was so thoughtful and sweet of him to get that for her. Maybe he wasn't so scary. Ellie had said he was basically a big marshmallow when it came to all the Littles. Looks really could be deceiving.

Angel handed the backpack to Leo. "There's pajamas in here for her and a pacifier. Her baby doll is also in there. She's wearing panties so she'll use the potty by herself. Call or text me if anything comes up and I'll be here right away."

Nora felt herself blush all over as Angel gave Leo instructions and told him about her pacifier and that she was wearing panties. It also made her tingly between her legs that the two men were having a conversation amongst themselves about her while she was right there. It made her feel very Little.

Leo nodded. "We'll be just fine. Be careful."

Angel grunted. "We will. Declan's men will be out front watching the house. Since all the girls are here, there are several of them out there."

Claire walked over and grabbed onto Leo's hand, smiling at Nora. "Hi, Nora. I don't know if you remember me. I'm Claire."

Nodding, Nora offered the woman a small smile. The woman was older, but she looked just as Little as the rest of the women. Ellie had told her Claire was Kylie's mom which she thought was so cool that both women had found their Daddies in the same family.

"Do you want to make bracelets with me? I have all the beads and everything. Daddy got me a whole set," Claire told her.

That sounded so fun. Looking up at Angel, he nodded

and smiled. "Go, have fun, baby girl. You have your phone so you can call or text me if you need me. I'll be back as soon as I can, okay?"

Nodding, she wrapped her arms around Angel's waist for a hug. He immediately scooped her up and hugged her close to him, pressing kisses into her neck. "You're safe here, baby girl."

All his reassurances meant the world to her. It was something so small, yet it helped her relax each time he told her she was safe. She trusted Angel and if he said she was safe, she was safe.

"Be careful, Daddy," she whispered into his ear.

He pulled back and smiled at her. "I will be very careful."

When he set her down on her feet, she hesitated to let go of his hand before she followed Claire over to the kitchen island where she had a whole set-up with beads and bobbles to make bracelets. She climbed up onto one of the stools and watched as Claire started stringing beads. The other woman didn't engage in conversation, just looked up and smiled warmly at Nora every once in a while.

Picking up the string, Nora started making a bracelet and they both sat quietly for a long time working on their masterpieces.

"That's so pretty. I love those colors together," Ellie said as she joined them.

Nora smiled at her best friend, leaning over to give her a side hug. "I missed you," she said quietly.

Ellie grinned. "I missed you, too. Don't worry, Angel and the rest of the guys will take care of Trevor and then we'll be able to have playdates and stuff."

Lucy, Addie, and Kylie all came and stood around the island, watching them.

"Daddy said he would build us a playground in the backyard," Lucy told them.

Addie bounced on her toes and clapped her hands. "That would be so fun! I bet Wolf will make you wear bubble wrap before he lets you play on it, though."

All the girls laughed. Lucy rolled her eyes and held her thumb and index finger up only millimeters apart. "Yeah, Daddy is just a tad bit overprotective."

Ava snorted as she walked up. "They're all a tad bit overprotective. Sheesh. I can't even go potty by myself because Daddy thinks I might slip and fall in the bathroom."

Brynn grinned. "Yeah, well, my Daddy put up a railing on my side of our bed so I won't roll off in the middle of the night even though he sleeps with his arms wrapped around me."

They all giggled again. Leo walked up with a stern look on his face making Nora worry he was going to yell at them all, causing her to automatically tense up.

Leo shook his head, a slow smile spreading across his face. "You girls all know your Daddies are only so overprotective because they all love you so much. We love all you girls and we'd be devastated if anything ever happened to any of you."

He wrapped his arm around Claire's shoulders and kissed the side of her head. The way Claire looked up at Leo was so full of love and respect, it was beautiful. It was obvious the man treated her like a princess. It seemed all the men treated these women like princesses. Maybe she needed to take a chance and trust them. But giving trust was a scary thing for her.

"I love all you Little girls," Leo said then looked directly at Nora. "Including you, sweetheart."

She felt heat spread through her as she lowered her

gaze from his, looking down at her hands. Hearing that someone loved her was so foreign. The only person she had ever heard those words from was Ellie.

When she glanced back up at Leo, he winked at her and moved his attention back to Claire.

BY TEN O'CLOCK, all the other women were asleep in various places in the living room while the last half of the movie they'd all chosen played. The only other person who was awake was Leo who had been cleaning up in the kitchen while they enjoyed their movie.

Needing to use the bathroom, Nora gently pushed Ellie off her, giggling silently as her friend slumped over the other way onto Emma's shoulder. She stood and headed toward the bathroom, stopping when she caught Leo watching her.

He smiled. "Go ahead, Little one. Do you need help?"

She quickly shook her head and tiptoed the rest of the way to the bathroom. When she was done and had washed her hands, she stepped out to find Leo lingering close by.

As soon as he saw her, he smiled warmly. "Are you worrying about your Daddy?"

Nodding, she fidgeted with the hem of her shirt.

"He'll be okay, sweet girl. Angel is strong and smart. He also cares very deeply for you so he wouldn't do anything to risk himself."

When she didn't say anything in response, he held his hand out. "How about I take you up to Claire's playroom and we read stories to take our mind off things?"

She eyed his large hand. Her first instinct was to shy away but Angel's reassuring words ran through her mind, and she found herself sliding her smaller hand into his. He led her upstairs and when they stepped into the playroom, she softly gasped as she looked around. The room was set up like a dream. Pastel colors and lace everywhere. Toys and books and anything any Little could ever dream of was in that room.

Leo went over to the bookshelf and took a moment to pull out several books before he went over to the oversized rocking chair and sat. He let her look around the room for a moment and when her eyes met his, he smiled and patted his lap. "Come here. Let's read."

She hesitated for several seconds but Leo just sat and patiently waited for her to make her way to him. When he reached out and lifted her onto his lap, she felt tense at first but as soon as he opened the storybook and started reading, she started to relax. By the third book, her eyes felt too heavy to keep open any longer.

22

ANGEL

He knew Salvatore would show up with many of his men. The man wasn't stupid and while he wasn't nearly as dangerous as Angel, his brothers, and Declan's men, he was still a drug dealer and participated in other illegal activities. Angel knew better than to underestimate anyone. You never walked into a situation without being prepared. Which was why, when Angel and his brothers walked into the warehouse, while it seemed as though there were only eight of them, there were actually a dozen more mafia men positioned right outside ready to come in and attack at a moment's notice.

Salvatore had six men with him as he entered the warehouse that was owned by Angel and his brothers. Standing front and center, Angel nodded as Salvatore walked up and shook hands with him first and then started shaking hands with his brothers, his men following suit.

"Angel. Good to see you. It's been a while," Salvatore said.

There had never been any kind of bad blood between him and the other man, and he hoped there wouldn't be after this meeting. But what he did hope was that he would get some of the answers he needed because it was irritating the fuck out of him that they hadn't found the fucknut that had hurt his baby girl.

"Nice to see you too, Luis. I hope all is well," Angel replied.

The older man nodded. "Beau said you needed my help with something, but the last I knew, you guys don't touch drugs or ass so what is it I can help you with?"

Angel had to swallow his rage at the ass comment. He'd known Salvatore was involved with drugs, but he wasn't aware he was dealing women and that shit just didn't fucking fly with him.

"I have a situation that I'm needing to handle and it seems like you might be involved with the situation. I'm hoping you'll be able to answer some questions for me and help me out."

Salvatore's eyes narrowed and his eyebrows pulled together. "What kind of situation?"

Holding up his phone with the screen facing Luis, Angel asked, "Do you know this guy?"

He could see the instant recognition on Luis's face before the man quickly schooled his expression. "What is your interest in this man?"

"This guy hurt my girl. And it seems as though he's coming and going from The Cage to do some sort of trans-action in the locker room. After watching the videos, it seems you're involved with this fucker. I want to know who he is," Angel explained.

Salvatore's face stayed expressionless. "You're sure about this?"

Angel nodded. "Yes, I'm fucking sure. He hurt *my* woman. Quite badly. And we have no way of knowing if he had or currently is hurting other women. He gave her a fake name. The only thing we know is he's a cop."

None of the men standing across from Angel and his brothers flinched at that, telling him they knew he was a cop.

"What kind of work are you having him do for you, Salvatore?" Angel asked.

The drug dealer shrugged. "He keeps me and my men out of trouble. And he has taken care of a few traitors for me."

He knew well enough to know that taken care of meant he'd killed them, so the man was essentially a hitman for Salvatore. Angel was starting to wonder just how dirty Salvatore was. Up until before this meeting, he'd only thought the man dealt some of the lighter drugs like weed and maybe some cocaine. Now he was questioning what all Salvatore was into.

"I also know that whether I tell you who he is or not, you'll find him and kill him. So I'm guessing you're wanting his name?" Salvatore asked.

Angel gave him a single nod. "It would be appreciated so my girl isn't living in fear every day. He planted a bug on her car so when she ran from him, he followed her. Then, he showed up at the gym the other day. Which also brings me to ask how that whole set up happened and why the hell you're doing transactions in *our* gym?"

Salvatore shifted slightly, looking a bit uncomfortable. "I met him at a fight. We got to talking and one thing led to another. I offered him a substantial amount of money to keep our name out of police records. Of course, I tested his loyalty before I approached him for bigger and better things. He's a detective, you see, so I knew he would know exactly how to do the job without getting caught. The man has made a fortune from me."

Beau shifted beside Angel. "So you thought doing deals at *my* gym was appropriate? Do I come into your fucking territory and do business?"

Salvatore shrugged. "My apologies, Beau. I guess I didn't really think it would hurt anyone. He was a member and I was a member so it just kind of worked out. I should have spoken with you first."

"Give us his name and we'll call it even," Angel offered.

Narrowing his eyes, Salvatore swallowed and looked to his men before looking back at Angel. "Brent Altwood. He's supposed to be doing a job for me tonight and when I get confirmation of that job being complete, I'm supposed to drop off the other half of the money at the gym for him to pick up."

Angel smiled. "Well, then, we look forward to you letting us know when to expect him at The Cage."

"Of course," Salvatore answered.

Nodding, Angel reached out and shook the man's hand. "Thank you for your cooperation. I regret to inform you that you'll need to find yourself a new hitman."

Salvatore nodded, his face still completely expressionless. "Understandable."

Angel nodded and Salvatore and his men turned to leave.

As they walked together toward the door, Beau cleared his throat. "Salvatore."

The drug dealer stopped and turned to look at Beau.

"If you ever do another deal inside my gym, my brothers and I will make you regret it," Beau said coldly.

Angel knew gangsters didn't take threats well. A threat to a criminal was like a challenge, but the smart ones knew when they were no match for something. He wasn't sure how smart Salvatore was.

The man furrowed his eyebrows and took a step toward Beau. "What is that supposed to mean?

Angel took a step forward. "That means we'll fucking kill you and every single one of your men. One by one. And you know we will if you fuck with us."

Salvatore stared at him for several seconds before he gave Angel a sharp nod and motioned for his men to keep going. Good thing the fucker was smart.

———

IT WAS after midnight when Angel and his brothers got back to Pop's house. They all entered the house quietly knowing the women were all more than likely sleeping. When they walked into the living room, Angel immediately searched out Nora, frowning when he didn't see her but then realized Pop wasn't there, either.

One by one, his brothers scooped up their sleeping Little girls to take home. Angel walked down the hall and climbed the stairs in search of his own Little girl. When he got to the second landing, he could see the soft glow of light coming from Claire's playroom.

He walked to the doorway and stopped when he looked inside the room and saw Nora sitting on Pop's lap, sound asleep while he rocked her.

Pop was still awake and smiled when he saw Angel. "She's the sweetest Little girl, Angel. The perfect addition to our family," Pop said softly.

Nodding, he walked into the room and gently lifted Nora into his arms. She let out a small noise of protest but quickly settled against Angel's chest.

"Daddy," she whispered.

"Yeah, baby girl. Daddy's got you. We're going home," he murmured.

Pop followed them downstairs and walked them to the front door. "I'll talk to you tomorrow, son. Night, sweetheart."

Nora shifted, lifting her head just slightly. "Night, Pop," she said quietly.

Angel's heart swelled and when he looked back at Pop, he was pretty sure the man had tears in his eyes as he waved goodbye.

As soon as they were back home, Angel took her right upstairs and into the bathroom, setting her on her feet in front of the toilet. Keeping one hand on her hip to keep her steady, he used his other to tug her leggings and panties down.

"Sit down, baby girl. Go potty one last time before bed."

Her eyes fluttered open, meeting his gaze. Keeping hold of her hip, he took one of her hands in his and helped guide her onto the toilet. When he went to step away, her hand tightened around his. "Don't go," she murmured.

Smiling to himself, he stayed right in front of her, smoothing his thumb over the back of her knuckles. Within a few seconds she started doing her business, and he was so proud of her for trusting him. He wanted their relationship to become so close she never wanted him to leave her alone. They would get there. Slowly but surely. He would have the patience for her.

When she was finished, he helped her up and took her to the vanity, standing behind her so she was trapped between his arms as he started washing her hands between his. She stared at him sleepily in the reflection of the mirror, smiling softly. "Did everything go okay?"

Nodding, he kept his eyes on hers. "Yeah, baby. We have more information. I don't want you to worry about it, though. Soon you'll be completely safe and you won't ever have to worry about being hurt ever again."

She nodded and didn't ask any other questions. As soon as he was finished helping her wash her hands, he lifted her up to sit on the counter then grabbed her toothbrush and toothpaste, squirting a bit onto the brush. When she went to reach for it, he shook his head. "Daddy will do it. Smile big for me."

For the next few minutes, he brushed her teeth in silence with her eyes watching him the entire time. After she spit, he filled up a small cup he had near the sink with water and held it up to her mouth. She tried to reach for that, too, but he shook his head making her instantly drop her hands back down.

Lifting her from the counter, he carried her into the bedroom and sat her on the edge of the bed. Not wanting to look for a pair of pajamas for her, he went to his dresser and pulled out a soft T-shirt. Walking back to her, he stood close and reached for her shirt, pulling it up over her head. As soon as her shirt was off, he could see her nipples pebble under the thin material of her bra.

Angel reached behind her and unsnapped the hooks, letting the bra fall down her arms so her heavy breasts hung freely in front of him. Her nipples were so pink and plump, he couldn't resist leaning over and capturing one in his mouth.

She moaned and immediately arched up, offering more of her breast to him. When he took more into his mouth and started sucking harder, she cried out. His cock was hard as a fucking rock inside his jeans.

"Daddy," she moaned.

Letting go of her breast with a light pop, he looked down at her. "What, my baby girl?"

She peered up at him from under her lashes, her green eyes practically begging. She was too shy to ask for what she wanted so he needed to make sure that if he continued what he was doing, she remembered she could stop it at any time.

"What's your safeword, Nora?"

Her pupils dilated and her tongue darted out to wet her lips. "Red."

"Good girl. And what are you going to do if you want me to stop at any time?"

He watched her chest rise and fall quickly.

"I'm going to say red," she said quietly.

Nodding, he reached out and gently tweaked her nipple. "Good girl. And will I be upset if you use your safeword?"

She shook her head. "No."

Smiling down at her, he captured her chin, smoothing his thumb over her jawline. "Never. I'll never be upset or angry if you use your safeword. It's there for a reason. So I'm going to keep doing what I was doing and if you need it to stop, you say that word, okay?"

She nodded. "Yes, Daddy."

Fuck. She was such a good girl. How he got so goddamn lucky to have her come into his life, he had no idea, but he was never going to take it for granted. She was so special. Unlike any other woman he'd met before. And knowing how hard it was for her to give him her trust made the giving of it an even more precious gift.

Lowering himself to his knees on the carpet in front of her, he slid his hands up her ribcage, smoothing his fingers over her delicate flesh as he made his way up to the heavy underside of her breasts. Cupping them in his hands, he smiled as they spilled out around his fingers. They were fucking beautiful.

Leaning forward, he took one of her nipples into his mouth while using his fingers to toy with her other nipple, tweaking it occasionally until she was moaning and crying out almost non-stop.

He could smell her arousal and while he would love to eat her all night long like she was his last dinner, he also really wanted to claim her with his cock. He'd need to get her good and ready though, otherwise it was very possible he'd hurt her. The last time he'd played with her pussy, just his two fingers had barely fit, and his cock was much thicker than that.

When she slid her hands up over his shoulders and scraped her nails gently over the back of his neck, he practically came right in his underwear. Pulling away from her breast, he looked up at her and smiled. "I'm going to take your pants and panties off and eat your tight little pussy until you're screaming and begging for me to stop and after that, I'm going to fuck you until we're both screaming together."

She was practically panting as she bobbed her head up and down. Pressing the palm of his hand to her shoulder, he pushed softly so she fell back against the bed. Hooking his fingers in both her pants and panties, he pulled them all the way down her legs, tossing them aside so she was spread out completely naked in front of him. Her creamy skin was flushed and her pussy glistened with her arousal. She was pure fucking honey and he couldn't wait another second to get his mouth on her.

Lowering his head, he captured her clit in his mouth, immediately sucking hard enough that she started screaming and lifting her upper body off the mattress as her hands raked through his short hair.

"Oh my God, please, please, please! Angel! Oh, God!"

Lifting his mouth from her, he gave her a wicked smile. "God can't save you here, baby girl. But I promise, your Angel will save you and protect you and make you come over and over again. You just be a good girl and let it all go. That's your only job right now."

He went back to what he was doing, licking and sucking every bit of wetness he could get, loving the taste of her sweetness. He could tell she was close as her body started tensing and she began grabbing hold of the bedding until her knuckles turned white. Sliding one hand up her tummy, he started toying with one of her nipples while he used the other hand to push one of her thighs even wider to the side, giving him more access. Those two things seemed to tip her over the edge because she suddenly started screaming and thrashing while calling out his name over and over.

When her explosion subsided, he grinned as he lapped at her pussy for several minutes while she calmed down, catching her breath while making cute little moaning noises.

"Daddy," she whimpered.

"Yes, baby girl?" he asked, his mouth still pressed against her core.

"Please... I need you."

There it was. His baby girl asking for what she needed. Normally he'd enjoy making her beg a little but not this time. This time he was going to give her exactly what she wanted when she wanted it because she deserved it and because he could hardly wait another moment to be inside her.

Getting to his feet, he stripped out of his clothes at a pace that probably should have been embarrassing, but he wasn't going to be embarrassed about how badly he wanted to make love to his girl.

He walked over to the nightstand and reached into the drawer to grab a condom before moving over to stand between her thighs. When he met her gaze, he nearly chuckled at the size of her eyes as she stared down at his cock.

"That's... um... that's really big," she murmured.

This time he did chuckle. "You're good for my ego, baby girl. But don't worry. I'm going to do whatever I can to make sure I don't hurt you."

She raised her gaze to his and visibly relaxed before him. "I trust you, Daddy."

His heart swelled at that admission. He was proud of her for being so brave, and was also completely touched that she trusted him to take care of her.

Leaning over her, he rested his forearms on either side of her head so his entire upper body was covering hers. Staring into her eyes, he kissed her lips gently, taking his time. Her hands slid all over his chest then his upper back, running her nails down until she reached the curve of his ass.

"I love you, Nora," he admitted.

Her eyes widened and he could see tears forming, making him question if he'd told her too early, but then she nodded. "I love you, too, Angel."

A tear slid from the corner of her eye so he leaned down and kissed the spot where it trailed. "I promise to always take care of you and treat you right, baby girl. Always. I'll never ever hurt you."

She nodded, her hands roaming back to his chest. "I know."

Reaching for the condom, he started to tear it open, but she grabbed his hand. "I'm clean and I'm on the shot. I haven't had sex for several months and I always made him use a condom."

Was she telling him she didn't want him to use the condom? Because holy fuck.

"I'm clean, too, baby. I haven't had sex in a while, and

got checked a few months ago. I can still use a condom, though."

She shook her head and reached for the packet in his hand, tossing it aside. Angel groaned as his cock throbbed even more for his sweet girl. Wrapping his fist around the base, he lined the head up with her entrance and hovered there as he lowered his head to kiss her again. She immediately started kissing him back, tightening her arms around his shoulders so she was pulling him closer to her.

Using his tongue, he nudged her mouth open and together they explored each other. Ever so slowly, he nudged his hips forward so the head of his cock breached her pussy. She whimpered into his mouth, sounding more like pleasure than pain so he pressed in a little more. Her pussy was so fucking tight and he knew he was stretching her with each little thrust forward, but she wrapped her legs around his hips and locked her ankles together, forcing him farther into her.

"Please! I need more. I need you," she cried out.

"I don't want to hurt you."

"I need more, Daddy. Please. I want it. I want you to stretch me and claim me. I want to be yours."

Furrowing his eyebrows, he stared down at her. "You already are mine."

"Then take me, Angel. Fuck me, please! Make it hurt. I want it."

Shit. He couldn't say no to that even if he wanted to and he didn't want to. He wanted to claim her. All of her. And he loved rough sex. Threading his fingers in her hair at the base of her neck, he closed his fists so her head was held steady and then thrust into her roughly, making her scream first and then moan.

"Again," she cried out.

Pulling almost all the way out, he thrust in again,

harder this time. Nora's nails scraped against his back as she cried out, her chest lifting up toward him in response as she started moving her hips to meet him thrust for thrust. It wouldn't take long for him to come. Shit, he was already riding on the edge, but he wanted to make sure she came again, too.

Taking one of her nipples into his mouth, he started fucking her hard and fast while sucking hard on her nipple. He could feel her pussy start to tense around his cock and knew she was close. Reaching between them, he flicked her clit several times, immediately sending her over the edge.

"Oh, fuck! Oh! Daddy! Yes!"

"That's my girl. Come all over my cock, baby. Fuck, you're so goddamn beautiful. I love seeing my cock disappear into your tight little pussy. Ugh, fuck, Daddy's going to come."

His own orgasm barreled through him all the way from the tips of his toes to the top of his head and he let out a low growl as he shot his seed into her pulsing pussy.

They lay together in silence, still connected as he pressed soft kisses all over her chest and neck. When she let out a soft contented sigh, he smiled and looked up at her to find a wide smile spread across her face.

"Hey, pretty girl," he murmured.

She opened her eyes to meet his gaze and her smile grew even wider. "Can we do that again?"

Throwing his head back, he laughed and looked down at her again. "You, Little girl, need to get some sleep. But I think in the morning we can do that again as long as you're not sore."

When she let out a long and dramatic sigh, he raised an eyebrow. "Is my sweet Little girl getting an attitude with me?"

Defiance flickered in her eyes and he couldn't even begin to describe how happy that made him.

"And if I was?" she asked quietly.

Tilting his head, he reached down and tapped her bottom. "Then maybe I'll have to warm your bottom to remind you to be a good girl."

Bringing her index finger up to her chin, she tapped on it as if she was thinking hard but then grinned. "Fine. I'll be a good girl. For now. Besides, I think I am a little sore."

Nodding, he slowly pulled out of her, hating that she winced as he did so. "I'll be right back, baby girl."

He quickly went into the bathroom and cleaned himself up before grabbing two washcloths, running them under hot water, then wringing them out. When he returned back to her, her eyes were closed and she had pulled a throw blanket over part of her body.

"Daddy's going to clean you up and then I have a hot towel to put between your legs for a few minutes to help soothe your pussy."

She mumbled something incoherent and he had a feeling she was already halfway asleep as he started doing his task. By the time he tossed both towels aside, she was snoring softly so he climbed into bed next to her and pulled the blankets up around them before pulling her as tight against his body as he could. It only took seconds before sleep came to him.

23

NORA

Waking up in Angel's arms was quickly becoming an addiction. He was so warm and the way he wrapped himself around her made her feel so safe. She hoped he would never stop holding her like that through the night. When she was in his arms, she actually got rest. Add in the multiple orgasms the night before and she was pretty sure she hadn't moved an inch all night long.

One of his large hands ran up the front of her, cupping her naked breast in his palm. "Morning, baby girl."

Her arousal instantly came to life at the sound of his deep, sleepy voice. That voice could seriously do things to a girl.

"Morning, Daddy."

Rolling her head back so she was looking up at him, she smiled softly. He was staring down at her and from the feel of his erection pressing into her bottom and the way he was looking at her, she knew he was just as aroused.

"How're you feeling? Sore?" he asked with a concerned look.

She shook her head. "I'm good, Daddy."

Wait, was she sore? Moving her hips slightly, she winced. Okay, maybe she was a little sore.

Angel furrowed his eyebrows at her. "Did you just lie to me, Little girl?"

Uh oh. Shoot.

"Uh…"

Before she could think of an excuse, Angel was sitting up with his back resting against the headboard and was pulling her over his naked lap. She immediately tensed, expecting a blow to come to her body somewhere, but as soon as her body went rigid, Angel froze.

"Baby, it's me, it's Daddy. I'm not going to hurt you. Look at me."

His worried yet soothing voice broke through her wall and she instantly relaxed and looked over at him. It was Angel. He wasn't going to hurt her. He would never hurt her.

As soon as her eyes met his, he nodded and smiled warmly. "There's my Little girl. I shouldn't have moved so suddenly. I should have told you what I was going to do first. I'm so sorry, baby. I wasn't thinking."

She nodded, her racing heart starting to slow. "It's okay. I… It was just an automatic reaction. I'm sorry."

Shaking his head, Angel stroked a hand over her back. "Don't be sorry, baby girl. It's Daddy's fault. I will remember next time not to just make a move without telling you first. The only thing I was going to do was pull you over my lap and give you a light and playful spanking for fibbing to me about being sore. You're not really in trouble, although lying to me in the future will get you in trouble. I just wanted to give you a bit of a spanking to get you used to being over my lap and also so I could start to learn how much pain you feel comfortable with."

Shoot. She was so foolish and weak. She'd messed it all up because she just couldn't get over her fear of everything and the irrational thought that people were out to harm her. Her head hung low, eyes averted from him, as her lower lip began to tremble.

Angel moved his hand to her hair and gave it a soft tug. "Hey. Look at me. Whatever you're thinking right now is not true."

Sniffling, she peeked at him from behind her curtain of hair hanging in front of her face. He reached out and brushed it away so she had nothing to hide behind.

"I ruined the moment," she whispered.

He stared at her for several seconds before he shook his head. "You didn't ruin anything, baby girl. Daddy is still going to spank your bottom for fibbing. This is going to be a light spanking and is not a true discipline spanking. I want to get you used to the feeling of how being spanked by me will feel. You always have your safeword if you need it, though. And this time, if you need me to stop, you can also just say stop. We're going to take it slow and I'm going to ask you what color you're at sometimes. If you're good, you say green, if you're unsure or starting to feel overwhelmed you say yellow, and if you want me to stop, you say red. But you can say those colors at any time as well. Understand?"

She nodded, feeling relieved that he was back in Daddy mode and not letting her overthink what she'd just done.

"What are you going to say if you want me to stop?" he asked, keeping his eyes pinned to hers.

"Red or stop."

He nodded and started moving her over his lap again, moving slower this time. His cock pressed against her hip and it made her happy inside to know he was still hard for her. One of his hands rested on her back while the other stroked her bare bottom.

"Just so we're clear, lying is against the rules. Lying to Daddy about something that has to do with your health or safety is even more against the rules. If I ask you a question in regards to your health, which includes how sore your pussy or body might be, or your safety, I expect honest answers. It's the only way I can be sure I'm taking the best care of you I can."

She nodded, her head resting against the soft comforter. Just being in this position over his lap made her squirm and she had to squeeze her thighs together, hoping to hide her growing arousal from him. Why did it turn her on so much to be in this position?

"This isn't going to be a super hard spanking but I am going to give you a few harder spanks to see how well you handle it. After we're done with this, Daddy is going to give you a bath, then we might revisit the sex idea. Here we go."

Before she could think, his hand landed on her bottom. Not hard but just hard enough to make her yelp then moan as the slight heat spread through her body.

Another smack to the other cheek but this time instead of being surprised, she'd been expecting it and the only sound she made was another moan. Who knew being spanked could be such a dang turn on.

"You're my beautiful girl. I might need to start putting you over my lap every night so you can get used to my touch and so I can remind you how wonderfully perfect and special you are."

His hand came down over and over, covering her entire bottom and while it was definitely warm, she wasn't uncomfortable. Well, not really. Her pussy was soaked and his erection that was pressed into her hip was just making it even worse.

After several minutes she was squirming over his lap, raising her bottom automatically to meet his hand. When his palm came down a bit harder, it took her by surprise, making her yelp and whimper as he brought it down again on her other cheek. He spanked her harder and faster until she was wiggling and crying out from the sting.

"Ouchie! Daddy!"

He paused. "What color?"

Without needing to think about it, she answered. "Green."

"Good girl." He resumed spanking her just as hard and fast until she was panting and squirming, feeling like a turned on mess over his lap.

A few seconds later he went harder, covering the sit spots between her upper thighs and bottom and while it stung immensely and she was crying out, she also felt like she was flying, and with every impact she felt a little more weight falling off her shoulders.

"What color, baby?"

"Ouchie! Green, Daddy!"

She was out of breath and squirming like crazy as his hand came down repeatedly on her bottom, but she didn't want it to stop. She needed this and she knew Angel wouldn't push her too far.

"I'm going to spank you harder, baby girl. This will be the hardest I'll ever spank you with my hand. You need to tell me immediately if it's too much," he told her.

She nodded. "'Kay."

His hand came down and she cried out, kicking her legs on the bed as it happened again. It stung and she was breathing hard but she wanted more. Needed more.

"What color, Nora?"

"Green!" she screamed.

He chuckled and continued spanking her with his iron palm. "I don't know if screaming green is very believable."

She giggled, then yelped and kicked her feet harder. "I... ouchie! I promise... ouchie! Green!"

Angel spanked her like that for several minutes and even though she was flying and everything felt like it was falling off her shoulders, she also felt a surge of emotions coming to the surface and pretty soon, she had tears running down her cheeks. As soon as she let out her first sob, Angel stopped spanking her and slowly pulled her up into his arms, rocking her and talking softly to her.

"Oh, my good girl. You did so good. Let it out, baby girl. Daddy's got you. I'm never letting you go, Nora. Never, ever."

The tears continued but the sobbing quickly subsided and she snuggled into his chest, letting herself cry. When her breathing returned to normal, Angel held the lavender pacifier up to her lips.

She felt so light and free. Like all the years of pain, and self-loathing, and trauma was just disappearing with each tear drop that rolled off her chin. She had no idea how long they sat there with him rocking her, but it felt like a long time and when he shifted, lifting her off the bed with him, she tilted her head back and looked up at him.

He smiled down at her so lovingly it took her breath away.

"Bath time for my Little girl," he murmured.

"Will you take a bath with me?"

"Of course."

———

"But I want to go with you."

Angel shook his head. "Absolutely not. No way are you coming to the gym when we know that fucker is going to show up."

Nora looked up at him, her shoulders hunched. "You won't let him hurt me. I just... I don't want you to get hurt."

He captured her chin in his large hand. "I'm not going to get hurt."

"What if he has a gun?"

The smile on Angel's face was pure evil. "I hope he does have a gun. I'll have three on my body alone plus about three dozen more in the gym between all the guys we'll have there."

A shiver ran through her. She almost felt bad for Trevor. Okay, no she didn't. She hoped he got everything he had coming to him and more.

"Baby, I need you to be a good girl and stay at Pop's with the rest of the girls where we know you'll all be safe. That way I can focus on what I need to do and then I can come home to you, safe and sound."

Letting out a sigh, she nodded. "Okay. But if you get hurt, I'm gonna be really mad at you."

Angel chuckled. "Okay, baby girl. If I get hurt, you can be mad at me. But I'm not going to get hurt so don't get your hopes up about the being mad at me part."

Nora stuck her tongue out at him. "Smarty pants."

He winked at her and continued packing clothes into her pink backpack. Angel had gotten a call earlier in the day that Trevor was going to be showing up at the gym to pick up the second part of his money so all the women were going to be dropped off at Pop's house again while Angel and his brothers, along with Declan and some of his men, went to the gym. She really couldn't wait for this situation with Trevor to be over.

Angel zipped the backpack and held out his hand for her. Taking hold of it, she followed him down the stairs and out of the house where the bodyguards met them and led them into the SUV to drive the thirty seconds to Pop's house. She definitely couldn't wait for the security guards to go away. They were perfectly kind to her, but they were intimidating as heck.

Pop opened the door as soon as they got out of the SUV and smiled at Nora as they approached. "Hey, sweet girl."

She smiled back at the older man. Even though she'd only spent a short amount of time with him, she'd decided she was safe with him. Angel wouldn't trust her in his care if she wasn't.

"Hi, Pop," she replied quietly.

She was pretty sure Pop's smile widened at her words and when she was close enough to him, he reached out and wrapped her up in a hug. It was an odd feeling because in a way, it felt like Pop was the dad she'd never had and it made her heart swell in her chest at that thought.

"I need to get going. Call or text me if you need anything. Either of you. I probably won't be back until tomorrow, baby girl. I want you to listen to Pop at bedtime and try to sleep, okay?"

She nodded and tried her best to put on a brave face even though she was feeling nervous about her Daddy getting hurt or worse. But he needed her to be strong and for him, she would be. "Okay, Daddy."

He leaned down and cupped her face, pressing several soft kisses to her lips. "I love you, Nora."

"I love you, too, Daddy."

24

ANGEL

He couldn't wait for this whole situation to be done and over. He and Nora had already lost too much time worrying about finding this fucker and keeping her safe. He was ready to move on from it and start his life with his baby girl.

Spanking her that morning had been intense. She took a lot more pain than he'd expected, and she'd slipped into subspace while he'd been spanking her the hardest. He knew some Littles who'd been abused in the past wanted or needed to feel more intense pain and he was okay providing that to her if that was truly what she needed. He would just make sure to check in with her often and have discussions with her to make sure he wasn't causing any emotional harm. The last thing he'd ever want to do would be to hurt his girl.

Pulling up to The Cage, he drove around back, not wanting his classic Buick Skylark to stick out like a sore thumb in the parking lot. Entering through the secure back door that only they had access to with their fingerprint, he made sure the door was closed before making his way down the hall to the room where everyone would meet before spreading throughout the gym.

All his brothers except Hawk and Wolf were in the room already along with Declan, Killian, and several of their men.

He shook Declan's hand, then Killian's. "Thanks for coming. We appreciate all the help you've provided."

Declan nodded. "We all work well together. You've definitely helped me out a time or two. I just can't wait to see you tear this fucker apart."

Nodding, he turned back toward the door when he heard it open, Hawk and Wolf both walking in together.

Hawk met his gaze and nodded.

"You got what I asked for?" Angel asked.

Wolf chuckled. "Delivered to the warehouse and practically wrapped in a bow. Or some rope and duct tape. Same thing. I'm looking forward to a fun filled night."

All the men in the room chuckled. They knew exactly what that meant. Wolf liked to see predators pay dearly for their sins. Not that Angel didn't. He was going to enjoy every second of the night.

"We don't know what time he'll be here to pick up the money, but Salvatore is going to message him at two and tell him he did the money drop. Usually, he comes almost immediately to pick up the bag," Angel explained.

Everyone nodded. They already knew the score and what their job was. Since they were in a public gym, they needed to make as little of a scene as possible. Angel knew he'd have to keep himself in check. He couldn't let out his rage until later. For the time being he needed to stay calm, cool, and collected so he didn't make any mistakes.

"Let's go avenge our girl," Hawk announced.

Angel smiled at his brother and nodded. "Let's go."

THEY DIDN'T HAVE to wait very long after Salvatore sent the message to Trevor or Brent or Stone or whatever the fucker's name was to show up at the gym. Colt was watching the parking lot surveillance so they knew as soon as he pulled up and got out of his car.

Angel made his way back to the locker room, checking all the stalls to make sure the room was empty before he got into place. Minutes passed by and he waited, sitting on the opposite side of the room from the locker that Salvatore had told him they used to exchange bags. As if on cue, Angel heard the door open and when he looked up, he saw his target.

Trevor met his gaze and smiled. "Oh, hey man."

Nodding toward him, Angel plastered on a friendly smile. "Hey, bro. Nice to see you. You come for a session?"

Trevor shook his head, turned toward the locker, then glanced back at Angel. "Not today. I just came for a quick workout between shifts."

Keeping his eye on him, Angel shrugged and nodded toward the lockers. "Cool, man. Alright, whenever you're ready, we can work out."

Out of the corner of his eye, Angel watched as Trevor turned toward the lockers and put the bag he'd carried in into the locker next to the locker that was supposed to have the money in it.

Standing from the bench, Angel started walking toward Trevor. "Let me give you my card so you can get a hold of me and schedule something."

Trevor feigned interest and turned toward Angel, reaching forward to take the card being held out to him. Just as Trevor closed his fingers around it, Angel shifted forward and brought up his other arm in a flash, grabbing him in a chokehold that would make him pass out within seconds.

Struggling against Angel's hold, Trevor gasped for air before he crumpled to the floor in a heap while Angel stood over him. Pulling out his phone, he quickly sent the confirmation text to his brothers and within seconds they filled the locker room.

Wolf quickly handcuffed Trevor's wrists as Angel and Hawk hoisted him up from the ground and carried him out to the hallway then out the back door to the waiting SUV.

As they threw Trevor onto the back seat, he began to stir, making incoherent noises. Angel quickly leaned in and barked, "Don't even think about it, motherfucker."

Trevor groaned in response, his eyes unfocused and struggling to stay open.

Hawk jumped in the driver's seat of the SUV while Knox climbed in the passenger side and Angel and Wolf sat in the back on either side of Trevor. Hawk began to drive out of the parking lot while Colt, Beau, Ash, and Maddox followed behind in a separate car to make sure they weren't being followed.

Angel reached into his pocket and pulled out a small syringe of clear liquid, tapping it with his fingernail. "This is going to put you out for a while," he explained to Trevor, "but don't worry. We're not going to hurt you—yet. Not until we wake you back up so you can be fully alert for all the shit I have in store for you."

Trevor's eyes widened with fear, but before he could say anything, Angel plunged the needle into his thigh and injected the liquid. Within seconds, Trevor's body went limp and he fell unconscious.

Angel just laughed as they sped through the city streets toward their destination.

GRABBING A CHAIR, Angel sat and smiled evilly at the two men before him. Both of them had started to stir, a sign that the drugs that had been injected into them were wearing off.

He waited for another half hour, watching the men as their eyes fluttered open and they began to struggle against the restraints they were in.

"Thanks so much for joining me today, gentlemen," Angel said loudly before turning his attention to the older man. "I trust my brothers treated you well and gave you comfortable accommodations while you've been waiting for me."

Several of his brothers had done the job of picking up Nora's father so Angel didn't have to take time away from her. Declan and Killian had assisted as well, making sure there wasn't a single loose end. The town that the older man lived in was probably mourning the death of their beloved doctor who "died" in his home due to a house fire. Of course, due to the fire department being occupied by another purposely lit fire at the other end of town, the body that was in the house was too burned to identify anything. Angel didn't know whose body was actually left in the house. All he knew was Declan had told him it was someone who deserved what he had coming and something about having the coroner on his payroll so if there was an autopsy on the leftover remains, it would be determined that it was her father in the fire. Mafia shit is basically what it sounded like so Angel didn't ask any questions.

Both Trevor and Nora's father squinted toward Angel, obviously trying to get their eyes to focus. When Trevor realized it was Angel, his eyes widened.

"What's going on? Where am I?" Nora's father asked.

Smiling at the men, Angel stood and walked closer. "Forgive my rudeness, I should introduce myself. I'm Angelo Cruz. You can just call me Angel, though."

The older man furrowed his eyebrows and struggled against the restraints again. "I don't know who you are! What the hell is going on?"

Angel shrugged. "You might not know who I am, but I know who you are. You're the sperm donor of my girl, Nora."

The man's eyes widened and at the same time, Trevor started sputtering. Looking toward the younger man, Angel raised an eyebrow. "Oh, I must have forgotten to mention to you that Nora was mine. I've been looking for you, Trevor. Or is it Stone? Or Michael? Or Brent?"

Trevor narrowed his eyes. "What the fuck is this, Angel?"

Looking from Trevor to her piece of shit father, Angel walked back to the chair, sat down again, and crossed his arms. "This... is the last night either of you will ever take another breath on earth."

Nora's dad struggled against the restraints again. "Do you know who I am? You won't get away with this."

Letting out a bark of laughter, Angel pulled a knife from his boot and walked over to the older man, running the sharp edge along his throat until it drew just the tiniest bit of blood. "Oh, I assure you we'll get away with this. And even if not, it would be worth it to make sure my girl was safe from either of you two fucks for the rest of her life."

"I'm a cop!" Trevor spewed.

Hawk stepped toward the two men and laughed. "You were a cop. You were stripped of your shield, which is why you left Seattle, and then you couldn't get hired anywhere else because of the shit you did as a cop back here. Nobody will look for you. Nobody will give a fuck that we're going to dismember your body and put you through a meat grinder. Not one fucking person will give two shits that the two of you no longer exist on this earth."

Both men's eyes widened as they struggled against their restraints. Angel just laughed and walked back to the supply table they had off to the side of the warehouse. He pulled on a pair of gloves before picking up a surgical saw and a clamp, carrying the items back to the two men.

Her father's face turned ghost white making Angel grin. "You know what these are, don't you, doc? Do you want to guess what I'm going to do with them?"

The older man didn't respond so Angel held up the saw. "I guess you'll just have to wait and see what kind of fun I'm going to have with it. It's going to be a long night, guys. Better get comfy."

All the men including Declan, Killian, and several of their men, except for the two fucks sitting before them, laughed as Angel turned on the saw.

ANGEL WALKED out of the warehouse the next morning feeling lighter than he'd felt in years. Maybe he was sick because of what he'd done and how much he'd enjoyed it but he didn't care. His girl was safe and while all the torture in the world wouldn't make up for the shit those fuckers had put her through, he was glad he hadn't just let them die easily.

All the men went back to the gym to shower and get rid of their bloody clothes. Declan and his men were already in the process of making sure everything was cleaned up nicely so no one would ever trace anything back to Angel or his brothers. Sometimes having friends in the mafia paid off.

When he finished showering and putting on fresh clothes, he headed for his car. He could hardly wait to get to Nora and wrap her up in his arms. They needed to celebrate, and he really felt like celebrating between her legs while she screamed out his name.

It was barely daylight when he walked into Pop's house with his brothers, but he could hear soft voices coming from the living room as they walked down the hall. Nora and Ellie were sitting up on the couch with their stuffies close by. As soon as Nora saw him, she leaped up and ran to him, throwing her entire body into his. He wrapped his arms around her, letting out a deep breath of relief to have her near him again. It always felt like he was suffocating whenever he wasn't near her. She'd become the very air he breathed.

"Daddy," she murmured.

He nuzzled her neck as his hand stroked up and down her back. "Hi, baby girl."

She pulled back and searched his face for a few seconds. "Did everything go okay?"

Nodding, he smiled. "Yeah, baby. Everything went great. You don't ever have to worry about them hurting you again."

Her eyebrows pulled together. "Them?"

"Trevor and your father."

Letting out a small gasp, tears filled her eyes and suddenly, she wrapped her arms around him tight. "Thank you, Daddy. Thank you, thank you, thank you. I love you so much."

Closing his eyes, he held her tight, kissing her shoulder several times. "I love you, too, baby. Let's go home, yeah?"

She nodded and he carried her out of the house, grabbing her backpack from the entryway as they left.

"Hey, Daddy?"

"Yeah, baby?"

"How does a polar bear build a house?"

A slow smiled spread as he walked toward their house. "I don't know. How?"

Nora giggled. "Igloos it together."

Angel laughed and tickled her side. "You're funny, Little girl."

The proud smile she wore on her face made his heart swell. It would take time but his girl was coming out of her shell and gaining confidence a bit at a time.

When they were inside, he took her straight upstairs to their bedroom and set her down on the bed. Without words, he slowly and gently started undressing her. Their eyes stayed locked on each other's the entire time and once she was naked, he stripped, too.

Her eyes flicked down to his bobbing cock and to his surprise, she reached out and grabbed hold of it, guiding it to her mouth as she leaned down to bring her lips around the crown. Angel groaned and rolled his head back as she swirled her tongue around the shaft. He wouldn't last being in her mouth. It was too hot and wet and fuck if she didn't look so damn beautiful as she sucked him down, opening her throat for him.

"Baby girl," he growled.

Opening her eyes, she looked up at him while keeping his cock in her mouth, and that sight alone was nearly enough to make him explode. Reaching out, he grabbed a fistful of her hair and gently pulled her head back, then leaned down and captured her mouth with his.

She whimpered into his mouth, bringing her fingers up to his chest. When she curled her fingers and ran her fingernails down his stomach, he grabbed hold of her hips and moved her roughly so she was farther back on the bed. Putting one knee on the mattress, he hovered over her as she leaned back, looking up at him with a smile stretched over her lips.

"I'm going to fuck you really hard and after, I'm going to make love to your beautiful body all day long," he told her.

Her eyes widened and when she nodded, he plunged his cock into her soaked pussy, making her cry out. Keeping his eyes locked on hers, he fucked her roughly, running his hands over her breasts, pinching the delicate flesh as he rocked his body against hers. When she wrapped a leg around one of his and started meeting his thrusts, he knew she was close. He was, too. Reaching between them, he slipped his fingers over her clit and flicked it several times until she was screaming out her orgasm, her pussy pulsing around him. His own orgasm exploded so intensely he nearly collapsed on top of her afterward. Instead, he managed to roll to his back and pull her on top of him, staying seated inside her.

They stayed like that for a long time and when his cock started hardening inside her again, she started grinding her hips against him. When she sat up on his cock while gazing down at him, she looked like a goddess, and he was pretty sure she felt like one with the way she started riding him.

"I love you, Nora."

She smiled, her hair falling over her shoulders as she rested her hands flat on his chest. Letting out a soft moan, she whispered. "I love you, too, Daddy."

25

NORA

TWO WEEKS LATER

"Daddy, we're gonna be late."

Angel ignored her and continued lapping at her pussy with his tongue. They'd been in bed together all day, fucking like bunnies, until they'd absolutely had to get up and get ready to go out for drinks at Maddox's club with the rest of the family.

He'd washed her from head to toe and by the time they'd stepped out of the shower, she felt like a pile of goo. Not that it mattered, she hadn't had to lift a finger to get herself ready for the night out. Angel had brushed out her hair, blow-dried it, then styled it in two high pigtails with bows at the base. After he was done with that, he'd dressed her in a pair of pink cotton panties that had tiny hearts on them and a pink cotton dress that made her feel Little but was also still appropriate to wear out in public.

As soon as he'd gotten her dressed, though, he'd practically tackled her to the bed, ripped her panties off, and started eating her pussy like a starved beast.

Lifting his head from her clit, he slid in one thick finger while he stared up at her with his dark gaze. "I don't give a fuck if we're late. They can have drinks without us. I want to make my girl scream again before we leave."

He curled his finger inside her and resumed sucking on her clit until she was slapping the bed and screaming out his name. Angel held her down and continued playing with her until her orgasm subsided and she was left panting and whimpering softly.

When he gently pulled his finger free, she watched as he brought it up to his mouth and licked it clean. For some reason she found it so hot when he did that. It was like he wanted every single last drop of her.

He stood and adjusted his cock in his jeans, smiling down at her. "Okay, now we can go."

Letting out a soft giggle, she shook her head at him. "You're silly."

The past two weeks had been absolute heaven. She'd resumed working regularly and Angel had, too, but he'd rearranged for all his clients to fly into Seattle instead of him traveling to them. She'd told him she could travel with him, but he'd refused and told her that giving her a stable routine and home were more important. It was really sweet, and he had been keeping her on a strict schedule of bedtimes and meal times which seemed to make her feel more secure than ever.

Tonight was going to be the first night she'd be allowed to stay up past her bedtime. Surprisingly, she wasn't panicking inside about going to the club. She knew Angel and the rest of his family wouldn't expect her to talk any more than she felt comfortable with so there was no pressure. Plus, since she'd learned that Maddox's Little girl was sometimes non-verbal, too, it made her feel a little less insecure about how quiet she was. She suspected she'd like to have a playdate with Brynn sometime. Well, she was actually looking forward to having a playdate with all the girls. Ellie was even working on getting a tea party scheduled for all of them that none of the men would be allowed to attend. Somehow, she suspected the men would still be there in one way or another. They were just a teensy bit overprotective, even with the danger of Trevor being over.

Angel helped her into her panties again before he knelt in front of her and slipped a pair of flat strappy sandals onto her feet. When he stood, he held out his hand and helped her slide off the edge of the bed, then grabbed her denim jacket and helped her into that.

There wasn't much he'd allowed her to do over the past couple of weeks. He bathed her, brushed her hair, fed her, cleaned up after her, dressed her, and pretty much everything in between. At first, she'd felt like he was doing everything and she wasn't doing anything to contribute to their relationship, but as each day passed, she'd started to realize that it honestly made him happy to do all those things for her. It was what made him feel fulfilled as a Daddy. He definitely made her feel completely spoiled and since that was something she'd never experienced, she was soaking it up.

It was nearly dark by the time they left the house and they were already almost a half hour late, but he didn't seem to care as he took his time buckling her into the passenger side of his Skylark. She loved riding in that car. The purr of the engine and the vibration of the power was such a turn on. Hmm, maybe she'd need to try to get him to fuck her in the back seat sometime. That sounded like fun.

He held her hand as they drove, running his thumb over the back of her knuckles. "I'm going to marry you one day soon, Little girl."

Heat spread through her entire body as she looked over at him. He'd told her several times that he was going to marry her one day and every time he said it, she could swear she fell for him a little more. How he could be so sure of her after only a few weeks she didn't know but then again, she was sure about him, and she'd been sure about him after only a few days.

"I can't wait for that day, Daddy."

When he parked the car in the VIP parking spots that were for Angel and his brothers, he got out and rounded the car to let her out. She'd learned quickly that she wasn't allowed to touch any door handles because that was his job.

Just as he closed the passenger door, the sound of squealing tires could be heard and Angel spun around looking in the direction of the noise. Before she could even turn her head to look where it was coming from, gunshots exploded into the night air. She could hear the bullets whistle by them right before Angel threw his body over hers, bringing her down to the ground.

She felt as if time had stopped right then and there as Angel shielded her body with his. A barrage of bullets echoed in the air and Angel returned fire, pushing himself up to return shots at whoever was shooting at them.

Angel's brothers flooded the parking lot, shouting. Some of them jumped into their cars while several rushed toward where they were lying on the ground while firing their own guns back at the attackers. As quickly as it began, the gunfire ended, and suddenly she felt something warm dripping on her leg. She turned to Angel, who was now raising himself up slightly, and saw a growing pool of red slowly soaking his shirt on his left side.

Panic took hold of her and before she knew it, she was up on her knees, screaming while tears streamed down her face as she pressed two hands firmly against the wound.

Knox, Maddox, Beau, Leo, and Hawk were right there and when Hawk tried to pull her away from Angel, she flailed and thrashed wildly, her fingernails leaving scratches along his arms. Her yells were desperate as she screamed at him to let her go until he finally did.

"Baby, it's okay. I'm fine," Angel reassured her as he handed his gun to one of his brothers.

She shook her head, her chest heaving and tears streaming down her face as she watched a river of blood flow from his body. Knox ripped off his shirt and handed it to Angel who hastily pressed it against the wound. Hawk looped an arm around her and tried again to lift her away from the horrific sight. She fought him, pounding at his chest and screaming for Angel.

"Baby girl, let Hawk take you to the car. We need to get out of here," Angel said sternly.

A broken cry escaped her lips as she let Hawk scoop her into his arms before he raced toward the car, his feet pounding on the pavement. Through bleary eyes, she watched as Beau and Knox carefully lifted Angel off the ground, supporting him as he limped to the car.

"The girls," Knox shouted.

Leo nodded. "I'll get them home. Maddox, is there an SUV in the back?"

Maddox nodded. "Yep. Here's the keys. Hawk, I'll call Tate and have him meet you at Angel's house."

Hawk nodded. "Thanks. Get the rest of our cars out of here."

"I'm on it," Maddox replied as he brought his phone up to his ear.

The men continued to give instructions to each other while Knox helped Angel lower himself into the passenger side of the car. Nora practically threw herself into the front seat, clinging to him.

"Daddy, you can't die," she sobbed.

Angel smiled at her and stroked her hair away from her face. "I'm not going to die, baby girl. The fuckers who shot me are going to die, but I'm not dying anytime soon. I don't even think there's a bullet in me. I think it was just a graze."

Somehow, she was pretty sure he was just saying that to make her calm down.

She sobbed harder. When Hawk got into the car, he turned toward her. "Nora, baby, get buckled."

Wanting to ignore Hawk, she looked at Angel who raised an eyebrow at her. "Get buckled, now, Little girl. My arms aren't injured, so I can still spank you."

Letting out a gasp, she sank into the back seat and quickly buckled herself in as Hawk started driving through the city.

"W-who was that?" she asked through sobs.

Angel looked back at her and then at Hawk. "It was Salvatore, wasn't it?"

Hawk nodded. "Yeah. I'm guessing he didn't like that we threatened him."

Shrugging, Angel leaned back in the seat. "I'm guessing he doesn't realize he just signed his own death warrant."

As they drove, Angel reached back between the seats and stroked her leg. "I'm going to be fine, baby girl."

She nodded but until she knew for sure, she was freaking out inside and all she wanted to do was crawl into her Daddy's lap where she felt the safest.

Just as they pulled into Angel's driveway, another car

pulled in next to them and she recognized the man as the same doctor that had checked her out when she'd first shown up at Hawk and Ellie's.

Hawk got out of the car and reached into the back, unbuckling Nora and pulling her into his arms as Angel got out on the other side.

"He's going to be okay, sweet girl. Your Daddy is tough and he's not ever going to let anything take him away from you," Hawk said quietly as he carried her up to the front door.

She nodded but didn't say anything. As soon as they were inside, she started wiggling until Hawk put her down. Angel was already ahead of them with Tate, so she ran down the hall into the kitchen where Tate was already digging supplies out of his bag.

The doctor looked up at her and smiled kindly. "Hey, Little one. I'm glad to see you all healed up. Looks like I get to fix up your Daddy. I probably won't be as gentle with him, though."

Hawk and Angel chuckled but Nora narrowed her eyes and put her hands on her hips. "You better not hurt my Daddy or I'll kill you."

All the men stared at her with wide eyes for several seconds before a slow smile spread across their faces. Tate chuckled. "Looks like you've been rubbing off on her, eh?" he asked Angel.

Angel winked at her. "She is the strongest Little girl I know. You heard her, Doc. You better not hurt me."

Tate pulled the blood soaked material away from the wound and lifted Angel's shirt making her gasp, her knees nearly giving out.

"Get her out of here. Nora, go with Hawk and listen to what he says. I mean it, Little girl," Angel said, more firmly than she'd ever heard him.

"He's going to be fine, Little one. I'm just going to get him patched up," Tate told her as Hawk reached out for her.

Tears fell down her cheeks as Hawk carried her through the house and up the stairs. She didn't fight him, though. Instead, she snuggled into his chest and cried.

When they were in the bedroom, Hawk carried her to the bed and set her down, kneeling in front of her so he wasn't looming over her. "You're being a very good girl. I know this is scary, but Angel is going to be fine. You just need to let the Doc take care of him and let me take care of you right now. As soon as Angel is stitched up, you'll be able to be with him, okay?"

She sniffled and nodded. "'Kay. Sorry I'm being bad."

Hawk smiled. "You're not being bad. You're worried about your Daddy and being a protective Little girl. I'm glad Angel has you. He's very lucky."

When she nodded again, he rose and looked around the room. "Point me in the direction of some pajamas."

Nora pointed toward the dresser, feeling herself blush as Hawk sifted through the drawer that held all her panties. When he turned around, he nodded toward the bathroom. "You need to shower. Can you shower by yourself or do you need help?"

Shaking her head, she slid off the bed and walked toward the bathroom, her legs still wobbling. "I'm okay."

The look on his face told her he knew she was bullshitting, but she wasn't about to have him give her a shower. When he started following her into the bathroom, she looked up at him in panic.

"You're still shaking. I'm not letting you shower by yourself. I'll keep my eyes closed but I'm not leaving you in there alone," he told her.

Letting out a sigh, she knew arguing with him would get her nowhere. "Ellie told me you were stubborn."

He chuckled and nodded. "When it comes to the health or safety of Ellie or any of the women in this family, I'm as stubborn as it gets. I care about you and I don't want anything to happen to you."

Her heart melted a little at that. She was pretty sure Hawk wasn't the type of guy to just go around telling people he cared about them so the fact he'd said it meant a lot.

The next ten minutes was awkward as Hawk sat on the closed toilet lid with his eyes closed while she undressed and showered. He asked her how she was doing several times and reminded her to hold onto the railing in the shower. Sheesh. And she thought Angel was protective.

After she shut the water off and dried herself, she wrapped the towel around her body and stepped out of the shower. "Okay. I'm covered."

Hawk opened his eyes and smiled. "Good girl. Feel better?"

Nibbling on her bottom lip, she shrugged. "I wanna see Daddy," she whispered.

He nodded and stood. "I know. Let's get you dressed and then we'll go down and see him. Do you want a diaper or panties?"

She was pretty sure her cheeks turned seventeen shades of red. Looking anywhere but at Hawk, she answered, "Panties."

Thankfully, Hawk let her dress by herself and once she was in her pajamas, he took her hand and led her downstairs. Angel's shirt was discarded and Tate was in the process of stitching up his wound. As soon as Angel saw her, his eyes lit up and he held out an arm for her to come to him.

Slowly and carefully, she walked into his embrace and

snuggled into his warmth as much as she could without jarring him.

"I'm okay, baby. The bullet didn't hit anything critical," Angel told her softly.

She nodded. "Daddy, all of you is critical. I need every single bit of you."

Angel smiled and nodded. "Okay, baby. I'll make sure to bring every single bit of me home to you."

26

ANGEL

Despite the burning pain in his side, Angel moved over to the couch and pulled Nora onto his lap. His brothers and Pop did the same with their Littles so all nine couples were spread around the living room.

"We have Salvatore," Ash announced.

Angel grinned. "Anyone else?"

Wolf nodded. "A couple of the other guys who were at the warehouse the other day. They didn't like that we threatened them."

Beau snorted. "I didn't like that they were paying a fucking hitman and cycling it through my gym."

Looking at Pop, Angel met his gaze. "Pop."

Leo nodded. "Of course. Do whatever needs to be done to keep this family safe. I'll stay here and keep the girls safe."

Nodding, Angel looked at Nora and stroked her face. She was exhausted and he suspected she was in shock. He hated having to leave her but once Salvatore and his gang

were taken care of, he'd be giving her his undivided attention. "Baby girl."

She smiled at him. "Go kill him, Daddy. Just don't get
shot again or I'll kill you myself."

He stared at her in shock. When she'd threatened Tate,
he'd been surprised but now he was just downright
shocked. "Baby girl."

"He hurt you. I can't kill him myself so you need to do it
so he can't hurt you again," she murmured.

Slowly nodding, he leaned his head down and kissed
her. "Will you please be a good girl for Pop while I'm gone?"

Letting out a sigh, she nodded and glanced over at Pop
and back at Angel. "Yes. I'll be good."

ADRENALINE HAD BEEN the only thing keeping him going
through the night. Now that Salvatore and the others they'd
captured were taken care of and he was going home to his
baby girl, exhaustion was setting in.

The rest of Salvatore's crew would need to be taken care
of in one way or another, but Declan had offered to handle
that. Turns out the Irish Mafia didn't appreciate the drug
dealer selling women in their city. Angel knew Declan and
his men did some really bad shit. Way worse than he and
his brothers ever did. But they never sold women and they
never hurt children so whatever else they did really didn't
matter to Angel. Although, it seemed as though Angel and
his brothers and the Irish Mafia were quickly becoming
some sort of partnership, doing favors for each other and
that was just fine. He trusted both Declan and Killian and
the other men of theirs seemed respectable as well. They'd
certainly taken their job of protecting all the girls seriously
and that meant more to Angel than anything else.

When he walked into his house with his brothers, it was quiet. It was still the middle of the night so all the Little girls should have been sleeping but when the men walked into the living room, all nine of the women turned their heads toward them.

Maddox chuckled and shook his head. "Should have known they wouldn't be sleeping. I'm surprised they were so quiet, though."

Kylie giggled. "Only because Pop threatened us with punishments if we didn't zip our lips and try to go to sleep."

"And yet, you're still talking and you're awake," Pop said from where he was stretched out on the couch.

Unable to stop his laughter, Angel shook his head. "You girls have exhausted Pop."

Emma snorted. "Nuh uh. Pop is just being dramatic. We were angels. We didn't even do anything naughty."

Somehow, Angel didn't quite believe that. Most likely it was only a few of the Little girls who were naughty while the others might have followed the lead. He was pretty sure Nora didn't have a naughty bone in her body.

"You think having a food fight with chocolate syrup and sprinkles isn't naughty?" Pop asked, sounding completely exasperated.

All the women giggled.

Nora was practically grinning from ear to ear and Angel really didn't give a shit if she'd been naughty because it was obvious she'd had fun with the other girls and his baby girl was so overdue for some fun.

Ash narrowed his eyes at Kylie. "Why do I feel like it was you who started the food fight?"

Kylie's mouth dropped open and she glared back at Ash. "It was not me! It was Ellie and Nora!"

Ellie gasped, shooting Kylie a look while Nora's eyes went as wide as saucers. Angel raised an eyebrow at his

Little girl and crooked his finger, signaling her to come to him.

Looking around nervously, she got up from her makeshift bed on the floor and hesitantly walked up to Angel, her hands moving to her backside. When she was only a few inches from him, he leaned down and looked her in the eye. "Did you start the food fight?"

Diverting her eyes away from him toward Ellie, she shifted nervously. Ellie started to speak but Angel held up his hand to stop her. "I asked Nora the question."

Nora looked up at him again and gave him a slight nod.

Unable to hide his smile, Angel grinned at her. "Did you get Pop really good?"

His Little girl broke out into a fit of giggles and nodded. "We all did. He looked like a chocolate sundae."

Letting out a bark of laughter, he scooped her up and hugged her close to him, nuzzling her neck. "That's my good girl."

Pop just grumbled and rolled his eyes. "I can already tell you're going to get away with murder," he said, pointing toward Nora.

She giggled some more and snuggled into Angel's chest, grinning at Pop who sent her a wink.

Life was pretty damn good, even if he had been shot only a few hours ago. He wouldn't change anything about his life. All the pain and anguish he'd experienced in his lifetime was worth it because if things had been different, he may not have ever met Nora and that would have been the worst thing of all.

27

NORA

"Close your eyes."

"Daddy, they're closed! They've been closed this entire time."

Chuckling, Angel put his hands on her biceps and gently led her somewhere. She really had no idea what was going on, but he'd told her he had a surprise for her. She'd never had anyone give her a surprise before so she was both excited and a little nervous. Some people loved being surprised and some people hated it. It could really go either way. She had a feeling that since it was coming from Angel, she would love it.

"Okay. Open."

Blinking her eyes open, she let out a soft gasp. Angel had mentioned giving her a playroom of her very own in the house but what she was looking at wasn't just any old playroom. It was soft and airy with shades of lavender and cream throughout, and as she looked around, she decided it almost felt magical.

"I wanted you to have your very own playroom. There are still things to add and you need more toys, but I want you to come shopping with me. You never really got to enjoy your childhood so I want you to have your room exactly how you want it."

Turning her head to look up at him, she noticed he looked a bit nervous. She looked back toward the perfect room and shook her head. "I can't imagine a room more perfect than this. You... you did this for me?"

Angel moved behind her and wrapped her up in his arms, her back to his front. "I had some help. Wolf, Maddox, Ash, and Pop helped. Brynn helped, too, by picking out the hippo toy for you over there on the bed."

Tears filled her eyes and she quickly dashed them away, not wanting anything to blur the beautiful sight in front of her. It was so perfect she didn't want to do anything to mess it up but at the same time, she also wanted to go in and explore everything.

Angel must have sensed her inner conflict because he started nudging her forward. "Go, baby. Look around."

Taking small steps, she walked around the entire room. To the left was a huge basket of toys and stuffies piled up and arranged neatly. She couldn't see everything, but it looked like a lot of baby dolls, blocks, stuffies, and Barbies. Running her hand over one of the baby doll's hair, she smiled as she caught a whiff of the soft baby powder scent. Taking another step, she came to a stop in front of a whiteboard sign that had *Nora's Rules* labeled at the top. Glancing at Angel, she felt her cheeks heat. He'd gone over rules with her and she knew every single one by heart, but having a place where they were written down made her feel so much more Little.

Slowly, she moved around the room, in complete awe of the beautiful white crib with a drop-down side and next to it a matching white changing table that was packed full of lotions and powders and clothes. She blushed when she saw the stack of colorful diapers tucked into one of the cubbies. He had really thought of everything. Next was a dresser that matched the crib and changing table and on top of it was a lamp that was shaped like a purple hippo at the base. It made her giggle at how adorable it was. There were also strings of twinkle lights strung up in swoops above the dresser that she'd be able to see whenever she was in the crib.

The lump in her throat continued to build as she looked around. There was nothing she could think of that would make it more perfect than it already was. The last thing she came to as she finished her circle around the room was a beautiful white bookcase that came up to her hip in height. On top of it was a picture book and the cover immediately caught her eye. The characters drawn on the front of it looked just like her and Angel. Looking up at the title, she gasped. Reaching out, she ran her fingers along the lettering that spelled out *An Angel for Nora*.

Glancing up at Angel who was leaning against the doorframe watching her, she felt a tear roll down her cheek. "What is this?"

He pushed off the doorframe and walked over to her, picking up the book. "It's a special book just for you."

Sucking in a deep breath, she eyed the book, then looked back up at his face. "Will you read it to me?"

Holding out his hand, he led her over to the large rocking chair that sat in the corner of the room and sat down. Reaching out, he pulled her onto his lap and positioned her so she was sitting up to see the pictures.

Opening the cover, he flipped the first couple of pages and started reading, "Once upon a time, there was a sweet Little princess named Nora. She was a brave Little girl who had been through so much in her short life. People were mean to her and even though she was brave, she was also very scared.

He turned the page. "One day, the princess needed help because her own family was terribly mean to her, but she was sure no one in the kingdom would care about her. The first day she walked through the gates of the kingdom, she was instantly surrounded by people who loved her. They accepted her for the special Little girl she was and with each day she spent in the kingdom, surrounded by love and friendship, she grew a little stronger and soon was blossoming like the most beautiful flower in the world."

He gave her time to look at the pictures before he turned each page.

"While she was in the kingdom, she always felt as though there was an Angel watching over her, making her feel safe and loved. One day, a prince came and the moment he said hello to her, she knew he was her guardian Angel. Princess Nora couldn't help but feel drawn to him, even though she was still afraid. As they spent more time together, she found herself falling deeper and deeper in love with him.

"The prince was equally smitten with Princess Nora. He thought she was the most beautiful princess he'd ever seen but her heart was just as beautiful as she was. Soon they were inseparable, and the prince and his family welcomed her into their family, giving her a type of love she'd never had before.

"The prince and the princess spent their days exploring the kingdom, going on adventures, and discovering new things together. The prince was always there to protect her, make her laugh, and hold her close when she felt scared or alone.

"One day, the prince took Nora to a secret spot in the kingdom where he had set up a special place just for her.

She'd never felt so loved and so special in her entire life. When the prince looked her in the eye, she knew he was her guardian Angel. And he knew she was the most precious person he'd ever known.

"Nora leaned into the prince's embrace and closed her eyes. She felt the warmth of his body against hers and the gentle thump of his heart. It was beating for her, and her alone. She felt safe and loved, as though all the troubles of the world had been lifted from her shoulders.

"The prince spoke softly, his voice almost a whisper. "Nora, I know that we have only known each other for a short time, but I cannot imagine a life without you. Will you do me the honor of becoming my wife?"

Nora's heart swelled with joy and she threw her arms around the prince, tears streaming down her face. "Yes!" she cried out.

"The prince wiped away her tears and placed a tender kiss on her forehead. I promise to love and cherish you for eternity," he said, holding her close.

"Princess Nora felt a sense of overwhelming happiness. She had never felt such intense love before, and she knew in her heart that this was meant to be. As she gazed into the prince's eyes, she saw the depth of his devotion and felt a sense of peace wash over her.

"Together, they sat and watched as the sun set over the kingdom, feeling the warm embrace of each other's arms. Nora knew she had found her guardian Angel, her protector, and her soulmate. She knew they would face challenges together, but with his love and support, they could conquer anything.

"The end."

Nora tried blinking back the tears that were already falling. "That was the sweetest book ever."

Angel shifted to the side slightly and a second later had

a small velvet box in his hand. Her eyes widened and when he opened it, she nearly screamed with excitement.

"I would get down on one knee, but I much prefer having you here, where I can touch you and hold you. Baby girl, that may have been a story, but it's our story and I love you so damn much. I never want to live a day without you. You're my everything, Little girl, and I want to protect you and love you and make you the happiest woman in the world. Every single thing in that book is true and even though you could do so much better than me, I promise I'll treat you like a princess and give you all of the love and support you could ever want or need. Will you please be my wife and make me the happiest man in the world?"

She nodded and threw her arms around his neck, sobbing into his shirt. "Yes! I love you. I never thought anyone would ever love me or treat me like you treat me. There is no better than you, Angel."

He held her against his chest for a long time, sometimes squeezing her a little too tight as they both let tears fall. His tears subsided quickly and when she looked up at him, she sniffled and smiled at him.

"Let me see your hand, baby girl."

Bringing her shaking hand up to his, she watched as he slid the ring onto her finger, letting another burst of happy tears break loose.

NORA WOULD NEVER UNDERSTAND why some days someone could feel on top of the world one day and rock bottom on other days. Ever since Angel had proposed, she'd practically been floating on air. Then suddenly, she woke up one morning a few days later and felt like the failure she'd always been told she was. She could still barely talk to anyone other than Angel and Ellie. She was still scared of pretty much everything. Work felt overwhelming and of course, she felt like it was because she was so stupid.

Angel was in his office on a conference call with a client on the east coast but when she went downstairs, he'd set out breakfast for her and a sippy cup of juice. Just one more reason she felt inadequate. He was always taking care of her and she did nothing in return for him.

Sitting at the kitchen island, she slumped over her bagel and sighed as the insults and mean words from her past ran through her mind. Suddenly feeling like doing anything besides eating, she left the bagel on the counter and made her way up to her playroom. She always felt at peace there. Maybe it would make her feel better to be in that space. Or at least it might put her in the right frame of mind.

Nora went directly to her toy box, dropping to her knees on the plush carpet, ready to immerse herself in make-believe. She pulled out three of her baby dolls and found some of their changes of clothes along with the pink plastic hairbrush that came with one of them.

Holding the doll with the curliest hair in one arm, she started brushing through her hair. Maybe she would give her pigtails. Or braids. She wasn't very good at braiding but she'd seen videos on how to do it. It couldn't be that hard. Right?

Once her doll's hair was sufficiently brushed, she set it on her lap and started to braid her hair. Well, attempted to braid was more like it. Nora's fingers kept moving the wrong way and her baby's hair kept springing free from the braid. After several minutes of trying, she started getting frustrated. Her frustration quickly morphed into anger and the next thing she knew, she threw the doll across the room.

"I'm so stupid! Stupid, stupid, stupid! Why am I so

worthless?" she cried out, throwing herself on her back onto the carpet.

"Excuse me?"

Her Daddy appeared above her as she stared up at the ceiling with a scowl. He didn't look very happy himself but she couldn't seem to find it in herself to care at that moment. She was worthless anyway and eventually, he would figure that out.

Putting his hands on his hips, he raised his eyebrows. "What did you just say, Little girl? Because I'm pretty sure I heard you call yourself terrible names and berate yourself, but I must have been hearing wrong because I know my amazing, strong, brave, and beautiful Little girl would never say such mean things about herself. Would she?"

Glaring up at him, she let out a huff. "I am stupid. And worthless. I can't even braid my doll's hair. I don't even make my own breakfast because I'm so needy and I sure as heck don't take care of you. So that makes me completely worthless."

She should have heard the warning siren going off based on the way her Daddy was looking at her. He was not happy. Nope. Not at all. Like not even close.

"We're going to have a long discussion that is going to take place with you bent over my knees. Stand up."

Shaking her head, she looked away from him. If she wasn't looking at him, maybe he'd leave her alone. Or decide she was too much work. That was more likely.

How wrong she was. Before she realized what was happening, Angel reached down and scooped her up in his arms, carrying her over to the big rocking chair. The way he carried her was tender and gentle but the expression on his face was thunderous.

She was still in her nightie and a pair of panties that Angel had dressed her in the night before after he'd given her a bath so when he put her over his lap, she knew her nightie wasn't covering her bottom.

"Daddy," she cried out.

"What is the rule about saying bad things about yourself?"

Letting out a sigh, tears filled her eyes. "I'm not s'posed to. But it's the truth. They were right about me."

He had one arm around her waist, holding her tight against him while his other hand rested on the curve of her bottom. "Who? Those motherfuckers who abused you? They weren't right about anything. They weren't even close to right. They abused you to feel good about themselves. You are amazing and smart and sweet. Baby girl, it hurts my heart to hear those words come out of your mouth. And talking badly about yourself or thinking badly about yourself is never allowed."

Tears were already falling to the floor and she had no fight left in her. Deep down she knew what he was telling her was true. She wasn't stupid. Or worthless. But years of hearing those words didn't just disappear overnight.

"I'm going to spank you now. Not because you're bad or stupid or any of those things. I'm going to spank you because I hope that in the future when you feel like thinking or talking badly about yourself, you will remember this conversation. Understand?"

She sniffled. "Yes."

His first swat startled her and she started reactively wiggling, but his hand landed again and again. This wasn't like the spanking he'd given her before. He wasn't spanking her really hard but he was spanking her rapidly, not giving her a chance to think about anything between swats.

Tears flowed but she stayed silent as he spanked her bottom for several minutes. When he paused, she thought it was over and started wiggling to get up, but he held her firmly, not letting her move.

"We're not done, Nora. I love you, baby girl, and my job as your Daddy is to protect you, even if it's from yourself."

Nodding, she sniffled. "I'm sorry," she whispered.

"I know, baby. But we're not done. I need you to remember this for a long time."

Before she could respond, he pulled her panties down to her thighs and started spanking her again, much harder this time. She started kicking her feet and crying out as the heat on her bottom turned to red, hot, stinging pain. Suddenly a sob broke loose and Angel instantly stopped spanking her and pulled her up into his arms as she sobbed loudly against his chest. It felt as though he'd broken her seal and now she couldn't stop sobbing.

Angel held her tightly, rocking her and whispering soft words of love to her. It felt like she cried for a long time and by the time her sobs stopped and she was a teary, snotty, blotchy faced mess, she felt completely drained, but her mind was silent. Those terrible thoughts she'd been having earlier were gone and she felt cleansed.

"Did something happen this morning that made you have those icky thoughts?" Angel finally asked.

She shuddered against him as she thought about the evil voices she'd had running through her mind. "Sometimes I hear my father and Trevor's voices calling me names."

His hand smoothed up and down her back. "I need you to do something for me when that happens."

"What?"

"I need you to come to me and tell me when those voices are running through your head. I need you to tell me right away so I can replace those voices with my own and build you up."

That sounded incredibly difficult. She wasn't all that great at communicating and while she trusted Angel completely, she still struggled with asking for things or telling him if something was bothering her.

"I can try," she murmured.

"Baby girl, have you ever gone to therapy?"

She shook her head. "No. I've avoided doctors completely."

He let out a soft sigh. "I understand why, but we need to work on that. You have to have regular check-ups and dental cleanings. But a therapist would be different than a doctor. I know a woman here in Seattle. Her name is Savannah and she is a sex-positive therapist. She is familiar with Littles and has extensive training in child-hood trauma and abuse. She's very kind and I think you would really like her. She might be able to help you work through some things that I don't have the knowledge on how to help you with. Would you be interested in meeting with her?"

Twisting her fingers in his shirt, she thought about that. Savannah sounded wonderful but Nora wasn't exactly very good about talking to strangers. But since she was a woman, maybe it would be easier. She hated the thought of going alone. What if the woman judged her?

"Would you go with me? Like into the room?" she asked quietly.

She hated how needy she sounded.

"Absolutely, baby girl. I will go to every session and you can sit on my lap the entire time if that makes you feel safer. Whatever you need, I will be there with you through it all, Little girl. You never have to face anything alone again."

And this was one of the millions of reasons why she loved this man so much. How had she gotten so lucky? She definitely needed to thank Ellie for having a part in the two of them meeting.

"Okay, Daddy. I think I'd like to try. Maybe she can help me."

He smiled down at her, his eyes soft, and she knew she'd made the right choice. She just hoped this therapist was as good as she sounded and hoped that maybe she could start to actually heal from her horrific past. In reality, she knew she had already started healing thanks to the love and support from Angel, but having a little help from another person might not be so bad.

"I love you, Nora. I'm so proud of you. You're my strong, beautiful, brave girl."

Every time he said those things, it felt like he chipped a little bit of her trauma away.

"I love you, too, Daddy."

EPILOGUE

THREE WEEKS LATER

NORA

I t was finally happening! Her first slumber party ever!
Ellie had organized it and all the Littles were going to
sleep over at Hawk and Ellie's while the men made
themselves scarce after they had family dinner together.
She had no doubts the men would be somewhere in the
house, probably with a dozen baby monitors surrounding
the Littles so they could keep tabs, but that was fine with
her. She'd prefer to have Angel around anyway.

She was still in awe at how quickly he'd become her
safe place and her home. It was a good thing they both
worked at home and whenever Angel had to go meet a
client at The Cage, he packed up her work stuff and

brought her with him. Beau had even set up a desk for her to work at in his office. She was worried about it being awkward to work in the same office as Beau, but he never expected her to talk to him and it hadn't felt awkward at all.

In the past three weeks since Angel had been shot, he'd taken her to see Savannah twice a week. The therapist was sweet and understanding and Angel had sat in on all her sessions. Sometimes she wondered if he would get tired of her having so many issues, but after one of her sessions with Savannah where she'd brought it up, Savannah had talked through that with both of them and by the end of the appointment, Nora felt much better about it and Angel had admitted the same worry about himself, which was just absurd since she loved him for exactly who he was.

"Daddy, can we go yet?"

Angel shot her an exasperated look. "We still have two hours before it's time to go. I need to go take a shower. You, Little girl, need to eat your lunch."

Dropping her shoulders, she stuck out her bottom lip in a pout. "Can I have cookies with my lunch?"

She'd talked him into buying a pack of cookies when they'd gone to the store, but he'd only let her have two of them so far. Big meanie. He was like the sugar police.

"If you eat all your lunch first, I will give you a cookie when I get out of the shower. You don't need a bunch of sugar right now. Somehow, I know Ellie is probably going to have a whole crapload of candy over there tonight."

Letting out a long, dramatic sigh, she nodded. "Fiiiiine."

The corners of his lips twitched and she was pretty sure he was trying not to smile. It seemed the few times she got sassy with him he seemed more amused than anything.

He quickly schooled his face as he always did and raised an eyebrow. "Or you can have no cookies."

"Nooooo."

"Then get to eating your lunch. I'll be back down in a few. I love you," he said as he leaned over to give her a kiss on the top of her head.

"Love you," she mumbled around the bite of sandwich she'd just taken.

She listened as Angel walked down the hall and started climbing the stairs. Maybe just one little cookie wouldn't hurt. He wouldn't notice that three cookies were gone instead of two. Besides, she was close to her period so her body needed extra sugar.

Sliding down from the stool, she tiptoed to the pantry and opened the door, looking at all the shelves of food. When her eyes landed on the cookies that were sitting on the top shelf, she grinned. Stepping into the tiny room, she closed the door behind her and reached up to the shelf. As soon as she had the package of cookies in her hand, she felt a thrill run through her. Did she realize how naughty this was? Of course. But that didn't stop her because she'd never really been naughty just to be naughty and it felt kind of good. It was like a secret that only she would know and her Daddy would never find out.

Lowering herself to the ground, she crossed her legs and peeled the top of the cookie package open, trying to make as little noise as possible. Not that it really mattered since he was up in their bedroom and that room was soundproofed.

Pulling one of the cookies out, she brought it up to her mouth just as the pantry door opened. She squealed and looked up to find her Daddy standing over her with a stern look. Doing the only thing she could think to do, she shoved the entire cookie into her mouth.

His eyes widened and he knelt down, reaching his hand out. "Spit it out, now."

Shaking her head, she started to chew the yummy goodness.

"One."

Shoot.

She knew counting never led to anything good. Every time Hawk started counting for Ellie, she almost always ended up getting her butt spanked.

"Spit it out. Two."

Fiddlesticks. Opening her mouth, she let the crumbles of chewed up cookie fall into his hand.

"All of it," he told her.

She opened her mouth wider and let the rest of the cookie fall out. Once he seemed satisfied, he stood and went over to the garbage, dropping the cookie inside. As he went over to the sink to wash his hands, she scrambled to her feet and took off. He couldn't spank her if he couldn't catch her.

Just as she rounded the railing to climb the stairs, she heard his booming voice.

"You can run, Little girl, but just know that each second it takes me to find you is an extra spanking on top of the spanking you already earned."

Freezing in her spot, she thought about it for a split second before she decided the threat of more spankings didn't scare her enough to stop her plan to hide, so she ran up the stairs and directly into her Little room. Looking around for a place to hide, she realized there wasn't anywhere she could go in the room. The closet was too full of stuff her Daddy had bought her to hide in there.

Spinning around, she went to run out of the room but was quickly brought to a halt when she ran into Angel's hard chest.

She offered him the most innocent smile she could

conjure up. "Oh, there you are. I was just coming to look for you."

The stern expression on his face told her he knew she was full of shit. And she totally was. But also, she was kind of having fun being naughty. Although now that he was picking her up and carrying her over toward the rocking chair, she was starting to second guess her choice.

"I'm sorry! I'll never eat another cookie. Never, ever, ever again! No more cookies," she rambled.

Angel set her on her feet between his legs so she was facing him, and the look on his face wasn't angry. He never seemed to get angry with her about anything which was something she was incredibly thankful for.

"Little girl, I never said you couldn't have a cookie, did I?"

She shook her head.

"What did I say?" he asked.

Letting out a deep breath, she dropped her shoulders. "That I could have one after I ate lunch."

He nodded. "And you decided you didn't want to obey what Daddy had said? Because one cookie wasn't enough, even though there's going to be a bunch of candy at your sleepover tonight?"

Shoot.

"Well, um, you see, I just thought that maybe if I ate a cookie first it would help me work up my appetite to eat my lunch."

Yeah. Smooth. Go with that.

Angel shook his head. "Okay, baby. If you want to go with that. Either way you're getting your bottom spanked and then you're going downstairs and eating your lunch."

Sticking out her bottom lip, she nodded. "Can I have a cookie after?"

He stared at her for several seconds before he nodded.

"After your spanking, if you eat all of your lunch you may still have one cookie."

"Okay."

Angel took her hand and guided her over his lap. She hadn't been spanked in weeks so in a way, she knew she needed it. Maybe that was why she'd decided to be naughty. Being naughty was more fun and much easier than asking for a spanking. He'd told her she could ask for one any time, but she certainly wasn't just going to ask.

His hand rested on her legging covered bottom while his other arm was draped over her keeping her in place. "If you need to use your safeword, you may."

"'Kay."

The first smack startled her. Even though she had the covering of her panties and leggings, his large hand still stung her bottom. When the second swat came, she yelped and started wiggling. These swats definitely weren't light.

He only spanked her for a couple of minutes before her entire bottom was heated and when he paused and pulled her pants and panties down, she knew she was in for it. Darn cookies. Why did they always have to taste so good? All sweet and chewy. Crumbly and delicious.

"I hope this will be a good lesson for you to obey Daddy next time."

Before she could respond, he started spanking her bare bottom and she immediately started kicking her legs.

"Ouchie! Owwie!"

Her poor bottom was starting to feel like it was on fire.

"I'm sorry, Daddy!"

She could feel the tears coming and it only took a few more swats before they spilled over. It wasn't even that she was crying over eating the cookie and disobeying her Daddy, although she did feel kind of bad about that. It was more so that with every swat, it felt like all the bad thoughts or feelings she'd had over the last few weeks were dissipating into thin air. Not that she'd had a ton because between going to see Savannah and her Daddy constantly building her up, she hadn't had hardly any bad thoughts about herself.

The spanking stopped as quickly as it started, and she realized she was now sobbing. Angel pulled her up and wrapped her in his arms, murmuring soft words to her.

"That's it, my girl. Let it all out. I think you needed this, didn't you?"

She nodded and sniffled as she let the tears fall freely. He brought a tissue up to her nose and started cleaning her face. She didn't even try to stop him because she knew he wouldn't let her do it so instead, she let him do what he loved most and that was taking care of her.

"I don't even know why I needed it. I haven't been feeling sad or anything really. At least I hadn't thought I was," she told him between sobs.

He stroked her back while he continued to rock her in his arms. "Baby girl, sometimes people just need a release. There doesn't even need to be anything especially wrong. Just the daily life of work, chores, thoughts, and emotions. It can all build up, even if it's not all bad, and sometimes a release is needed. That's why I go beat the shit out of Hawk in the gym. Because it gives me what I need to let it all go."

Nodding, she sniffed and he reached down with a clean tissue and wiped her nose again.

"How did you know I went into the pantry?"

Angel chuckled. "Baby girl, you know I have baby monitors with cameras in every room of this house. You knew I'd be able to see you go in there. Whether you realize it or not, you were hoping to get caught. And that's perfectly okay. I know it can be hard to ask for a spanking so if being naughty is easier for you, that's okay with me. Besides, I like seeing you be a little mischievous. It means you feel safe here."

She nodded. "I always feel safe with you."

"I'm so glad. I'm doing my job as Daddy right then."

They sat in silence for a few more minutes before he helped her up from his lap and pulled her panties and leggings back into place. "Come on. Daddy will come down and feed you and then you can come sit in the bathroom and play with your dolls while I shower. We have a slumber party to get to."

Grinning, she nodded and took the hand he held out for her.

ANGEL

DAMN, he was so lucky. Sitting around the dinner table with his entire family and his Little girl. Life could be a funny thing sometimes. The last thing he'd ever thought would happen would be that he and all his brothers and Pop would find the perfect women for them. When you come from a dark background, it's hard to see the light at the end of the tunnel, but the thing with a tunnel is there's always an opening at the end and there's the light when you start to least expect it.

Nora was his light. She was his everything and though he knew she deserved so much better than him, he would make himself a better man every single day for the rest of his life just so he was worthy of her.

Looking around, he watched as Knox screwed on the lid to Addie's sippy cup, Ash dished up some food onto Kylie's plate, Beau held a of spoonful of potatoes up to Emma's mouth, Wolf had Lucy on his lap while they both ate from the same plate, Pop was whispering something into Claire's ear that had her grinning, Maddox was blowing on Brynn's food, Colt was tucking a napkin onto Ava's lap, and Hawk was smiling lovingly down at Ellie. Running his thumb over the back of Nora's knuckles, he brought her hand up to his mouth and kissed the back of it. There was so much damn love in this room you could feel it and it made Angel feel emotional. Closing his eyes, he briefly thought of his mom and smiled to himself as the beauty of her face floated by in his mind. She was in a better place now and it gave him peace knowing that.

Pop cleared his throat and stood. "Things have been so crazy lately that we haven't been at family dinner all together in a few weeks. I know I always say sappy things when we eat together but as I look around this table, at my family, I can't help but feel so incredibly blessed. I may not have had the privilege to raise most of you from birth, but it's been my privilege to have you all join my family. I love each and every one of you and I'm so proud of the men all you boys have become, and I'm so proud of all of these strong women who sit around this table and have also let me become their Pop. I'm also incredibly blessed to have found this amazing woman right next to me who loves me unconditionally.

"Life may not always be perfect, and we'll all have our ups and downs, but we'll always be family and we'll always get through things together. As much as you may feel like Ma and I saved you boys, I want you to know that you've all saved me, too. I love you all. So damn much. To family," he finished, choking up slightly at the end.

Everyone raised their drinks at the same time. "To family!"

Wolf grabbed his napkin and dabbed his eyes. "Fuck, can we make these dinners a little less emotional? There needs to be a rule or something on Pop's toasts about not making me cry."

The entire room burst out into laughter while Wolf grinned and finished wiping his eyes before he gave everyone the finger. "I love you guys."

Angel grinned. "We love you, too, Wolfie."

Lucy giggled and snuggled in closer to Wolf's chest.

"Okay, let's finish eating before everything gets cold," Pop said, motioning around the table.

The rest of dinner was loud and entertaining. Both Emma and Kylie were threatened with spankings at least a handful of times. Nora ended up on Angel's lap while he fed her and himself between her bites. It was beautiful watching how easily everyone flowed together.

After dinner, the men cleaned up the kitchen while the Littles all went up to Ellie's nursery to change into their pajamas. Hawk set up the "candy buffet" Ellie had requested for the sleepover and Angel grimaced when he saw how much candy he put out. It was only one night though, so he guessed that wouldn't be terrible. He just had a feeling all the Littles would be bouncing off the walls half the night while getting into mischief.

When the women came back downstairs in all their frilly, adorable pajamas with all different kinds of sayings and pictures on them, the men were shooed out of girls' night. They weren't going far, though. Hawk had set up video games in his den so they could play games and drink beer and keep an eye on the Littles' antics.

He wrapped his arms around Nora and kissed the top of her head. "I love you, Little girl. Be good and have fun. You know where I am if you need me."

She nodded and smiled up at him, lifting onto her

tiptoes to give him a kiss. "I love you, Daddy. Don't worry, I'll be fine."

Grinning down at her, he tapped her nose. "I know you will be. Have fun and as long as you're safe, don't be too good."

Giggling, she threw her arms around his waist and sighed as she rested her head on his chest. "Thank you, Daddy. For everything. You saved me."

Swallowing the lump forming in his throat, he wrapped his arms around her and squeezed her tight. "We saved each other, Little one."

When they finally released each other, he was surprised when Nora pushed him toward the den. He made her giggle when he anchored himself and she wasn't able to push him any farther.

"Daddyyyyy," she whined.

Laughing, he kissed her one last time before he went into the den where the rest of his brothers and Pop were already sitting on couches with controllers in their hands. He sat down in the only available seat, next to Hawk, and leaned back against the cushions feeling so light inside.

Beau grinned at the rest of them. "You know it's only a matter of time before they decide to be naughty."

Angel snorted. "I'm counting on it. Nora needs to be a little naughty, though. It's good for her."

Knox nodded. "It's good for all of them. They know they're safe to be themselves."

Everyone agreed with grunts and nods and just as they were about to start a game, they heard the sounds of squeals and screams coming from the other room. It sounded like a pillow fight had broken out.

"Well, that happened a lot quicker than expected," Beau said with a grin.

Angel stood and chuckled. "Let's go bust some butts."

ALSO BY KATE OLIVER

PLEASE LEAVE A REVIEW!

It would mean so much to me if you would take a brief moment to leave a rating and/or a review on this book. It helps other readers find me. Thank you for your support!

-Kate